# SEGOVIA

*A Celebration of the Man and His Music*

Frontispiece: Andrés Segovia.
Photograph by the author — Madrid, June 1982.

# Segovia

## A Celebration
## of the Man and his Music
by
### GRAHAM WADE

c . 1

ALLISON & BUSBY
LONDON · NEW YORK

*Also by Graham Wade*

Guitar Method Volumes I and II (with recorded cassettes)
   (International Correspondence Schools, London)
Traditions of the Classical Guitar
Your Book of the Guitar
The Shape of Music

First published 1983
by Allison & Busby Limited
6a Noel Street
London W1V 3RB
and distributed in the USA 1983 by
Schocken Books Inc.
200 Madison Avenue
New York, NY 10016

Copyright © Graham Wade 1983

*British Library Cataloguing in Publication Data*
Wade, Graham
   Segovia: a celebration of the man and his music
   1.  Segovia, Andrés    2.  Guitarists—
      Spain—Biography
   I.  Title
   787.6'1'0924        ML419.S4

ISBN 0-85031-491-7
ISBN 0-85031-492-5-Pbk


Set in 10/11 Bembo by
Alan Sutton Publishing Ltd., Gloucester.
Printed in Great Britain by The Camelot Press, Southampton.

# CONTENTS

*FOR ANDRÉS SEGOVIA*

# ACKNOWLEDGEMENTS

The author would like to express his deep appreciation for all those who have provided encouragement and help in the writing of this book. In particular my thanks are due to Andrés Segovia. I would also like to thank those international musicians who responded to my request for birthday tributes to Segovia.

Thanks are due also: to Alberto López Poveda, to Nicholas Reed, Librarian of the City of Leeds College of Music, whose unstinting efforts on my behalf were invaluable, to John Mills, Els Breukers and Arnie Brown, for supplying much fascinating material and information about Segovia's recitals in Europe and the USA, to Robin Pearson of the Spanish Guitar Centre, Nottingham, for advice about Segovia's editions, to Melvyn Mountain for help and advice with photographic matters, and to Bill Swainson for his indispensable editorial presence. The efforts of my wife Elizabeth, in research, preparation of the manuscript, and the tasks of typing, checking and editing, over many months, showed devotion and endurance well beyond the call of duty, without which the task could never have been completed.

Grateful acknowledgement for the use of various quoted material is due to:

Andrés Segovia; Marion Boyars Ltd, London; Macmillan Publishing Co., New York; J.M. Dent Ltd, London; Bernard Gavoty, René Kister, Geneva; Peter Neville, Barrie & Jenkins Ltd, London; Arthur Hedley; Harold C. Schonberg, Victor Gollancz Ltd, London; Arthur Rubinstein and Jonathan Cape Ltd, London; the Decca Recording Company; Vladimir Bobri and Guitar Review, New York; Columbia Music Ltd, Washington D.C., Belwin Mills, Charles Duncan and Summy-Birchard; the *Daily Express*, London; the *Observer*, London; *The Times*, London; the *Chicago Sun-Times*, Chicago; The *International Herald Tribune*, Paris; Yehudi Menuhin, Macdonald General Books Ltd, London; Max Harrison; Philip Purser; Stephen Walsh and Keith Horner;

the BBC, Julian Bream; Museum Press, London; D.E. Pohren and the Society of Spanish Studies, Madrid, Musical New Services, Guitar House, Bimport, Shaftesbury, Dorset; the *Guardian*, London; Constable and Co. Ltd, London; the Souvenir Press; *Newsweek*, New York; *Reader's Digest*, New York; Alfred A. Knopf Inc., Edward B. Marks Corp., New York.

# PREFACE

THIS BOOK was written to celebrate the ninetieth anniversary of the birth of Andrés Segovia. In June 1982, he invited me to visit him in Madrid to discuss the project, and there gave me permission to write such a book, though he did not wish it to be too biographical as he intends to publish further volumes of his autobiography.

At the time Segovia was preparing to go to Japan where he was to play several concerts. He had ready three recital programmes, each containing substantial works, and was looking forward to visiting a country which he likes very much and where he first played in 1929. That a man of eighty-nine should possess so much vigour, enthusiasm and spontaneity did not seem extraordinary at the time. What is extraordinary for others has for decades been part of Segovia's normal existence. Most people approaching ninety have the physical and mental capacity to do very little; Segovia continues with his career, pursuing different fingerings for well-known pieces, learning new compositions, and taking the guitar to his public.

In this book I have attempted to discuss certain aspects of Segovia's background and development which have previously been neglected; the actual tangible achievements — recordings, editions of music and a representative selection of recital programmes — are set out so that we can contemplate the sheer creative energy of Segovia's ninety years in objective terms.

There are many great guitarists in the world today and many will be seen in the future; Andrés Segovia's legacy has made them possible.

GRAHAM WADE
August 1982

Besides, he deeply desired to live to a ripe old age, for he believed that only the artist to whom it has been granted to be fruitful on all stages of our human scene, can be really great, or universal, or worthy of honour.

*Thomas Mann*

Nimmer wird sein Ruhm verhallen,
Ehe nicht die letzte Saite,
Schnarrend losspringt von der letzten
Andalusischen Gitarre.

*Never will his fame diminish,*
*Not until the last string*
*Harshly breaks from the last*
*Andalusian guitar.*

**(from a tribute to another great man of Granada)**
*Heinrich Heine*

Allow me to say with pride that the guitar by being deeply Spanish is becoming universal. Spain took the guitar because the Spaniard has so rich an individuality that he is a society in himself, and the guitar by her rich polyphonies and tone colours is an orchestra in itself.

*Andrés Segovia*

# 1

# SEGOVIA AND THE TWENTIETH CENTURY

THIS BOOK is a celebration of one of the world's great instrumentalists — Andrés Segovia. In his lifetime, as the founding father of the modern guitar movement, Segovia has established not only a new repertoire and a new status for a hitherto neglected instrument, but also is representative of that élite community of artists whose work in the twentieth century has spoken for universal artistic values.

Through many turbulent decades, including times of civil and world war until the present era when nuclear weapons seem poised for holocaust, Segovia's art, like that of such instrumentalists as Casals, Heifetz, Horowitz and Rubinstein, has stood for order in a world of chaos.

With great artists it is the durable, ever renewing quality of their inspiration which commands the allegiance of their public. For Segovia, audiences have been willing to come to terms with the most intimate musical sounds emerging from the guitar. In a noisy age his ability to persuade us to listen carefully for fine distinctions of tone and dynamics just within the range of audibility is in itself something remarkable.

Twentieth century European culture has found it necessary to deal with the collapse of traditional values and the apparent shattering of continuity. In literature, music and the visual arts, the creative artists of stature, whether T.S. Eliot or Picasso, Schoenberg or Kafka, Joyce or Stravinsky, have explored fragmentation, the breaking of old moulds. The impact of such horrific events as the Somme, Guernica, Belsen and Hiroshima, has made a creative response to experience traumatic. Under such psychological stress, often intensified by the pressure of living in a dictatorship or totalitarian society, the lives of many artists have been blighted or destroyed. The deaths of Federico García Lorca and Osip Mandelstam, the muzzling of Pasternak and Shostakovich, the exile of Antonio Machado, Picasso, Casals, Juan Ramón Jiménez and Solzhenitsyn, are a few examples from an interminable list.

Andrés Segovia, as one of the great recreative artists, has not escaped the pressures of the twentieth century, and experienced himself the turmoil of the Spanish Civil War resulting in his departure from his homeland for sixteen years. Yet Segovia's art, instead of mirroring disquiet, has chosen another path. His pursuit of musical beauty as he understands it is so much a part of his own nature, so original and so profound, that it is itself a testimony to an inner truth.

In over seventy years of giving recitals, his art has endured as spontaneous and untarnished as when he set out on the journey. In his quest he has neither wavered nor been deflected by events or false trails. On every side more sensational and extreme artistic movements have flared like comets, then vanished. Despite rapid and frequent changes of fashion and taste, Segovia's audiences of all ages and nationalities have retained their trust in him and in what he has to say. His stamina and longevity have reinforced his position as one of those rare figures who has kept faith with his art and with us.

Nowadays the classical guitar has moved onwards as new generations of players and composers, following Segovia's example, take up the challenges the instrument offers. Great guitarists such as Alirio Diaz, Julian Bream and John Williams acknowledge the original debt they owe to Segovia in terms of inspiration and repertoire. Each of them has advanced into new musical territory, creating their own characteristic sound and a personal artistic credo. World wide, teachers, arrangers and transcribers and the instrument's scholars and historians pursue careers made possible by Segovia's pioneering endeavours on the guitar's behalf.

This book is a small repayment of the debt owed to Andrés Segovia. Human memory is regrettably short and gratitude not a particularly enduring quality. Each generation tends to take for granted what it finds as if that is the natural order of things. But if Teilhard de Chardin's remark that "Everything is the sum of the past and nothing is comprehensible except through its history" is true, then it is clearly impossible to understand the classical guitar as it exists today without a proper awareness of Segovia's role in its development.

This and the following photographs were taken by the author in Segovia's apartment, Madrid, June 1982.

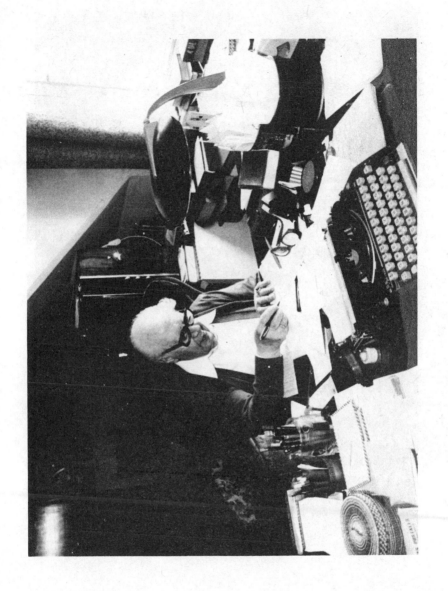

# 2

# TRIBUTES TO SEGOVIA

THE FOLLOWING tributes are from some of the world's leading musicians. Their discerning and generous insights extend to Segovia's personality as well as to his musical achievements. It is particularly appropriate that the greetings should come from the whole world of music for it has always been Segovia's desire that the guitar should be acknowledged and respected by all musicians. These tributes bear witness that such a task has been truly accomplished.

In order to realize the gigantic achievement of Andrés Segovia, it suffices to compare how the world was before him and what it is now. Then, there was an instrument used for the accompaniment of folk songs. Now, myriads of musicians use it to express beauty, and concert halls are filled with lovers of that instrument and the magic it creates. As in a fairy tale, the prince fell in love with the beautiful peasant girl and made her a queen.

It is easy to be wise after the event. We know that this achievement needed the touch of greatness, and we know that Segovia is great. One needs to be great to fight that battle alone — and win. But those of us lucky enough to know him personally have had hundreds of occasions to witness the combination of pride and humility which makes a great artist and a great man. One such occasion occurred three years ago when he greeted me in his hotel suite, his face full of happiness and said, "How wonderful! I have found a new fingering for this passage. So far it only went well at home. But yesterday also in concert!" (. . . Shall we ever know what "well" means for him? . . .).

Due to his friendship with my family he has always been like a father to me, an unfailing source of advice and help.

But also for so many others. His artistic descendants are already countless. Yes, we only need to look at the world before and after!

Thank you, Andrés. . . .

JOAQUÍN ACHÚCARRO

Bilbao


Dear Andrés Segovia,

Many things in the world have changed since you gave your first recital at the beginning of this century. Modern means of transport now allow a musician to perform in Madrid one day and in New York the next; massive publicity techniques create "stars" overnight who in this competitive, sometimes cruel world fall almost as quickly as they have risen.

But you have withstood the ever-increasing demands made on international artists and continue to grace stages all over the world, entrancing millions of those fortunate enough to hear you live, and delighting others by your radio broadcasts and gramophone records.

There is of course that magic which is unique to your playing; but underneath there also lies an honest man with real integrity and great musicianship. We applaud you wholeheartedly for your supreme contribution to Music and look forward to what we know you still have in store for us.

Very best wishes,

AMADEUS QUARTET

Norbert Brainin        Peter Schidlof
Siegmund Nissel        Martin Lovett

London


To say that Andrés Segovia revolutionized our thinking about the guitar in our time is only one aspect of why he will be remembered. Better, he will be also remembered as a great artist who transformed and recreated music to make it live anew on his chosen instrument.

CLAUDIO ARRAU

New York

Segovia is a peerless and unique artist; his art with its rare qualities of sincerity and humanity, is an example to all of us.

VLADIMIR ASHKENAZY

Segovia has an astonishing power of communicating with his audience. It is many years now since I heard him, but I can distinctly remember not only what he played but how he played certain phrases. As a performer he has both charm and warmth. I think of him not only with gratitude but with gratitude and affection.

SIR LENNOX BERKELEY

London

Heartiest congratulations to Maestro Andrés Segovia, a unique magical artist. It gives me an enormous pleasure to contribute these few lines, with great emotion and enormous admiration, which is shared throughout the world.

SHURA CHERKASSKY

Through their works composers may find immortality, in some cases perhaps more prosperously than during their lifetimes; performers survive only through their recordings — and these may in time become unavailable. It is also the way of the world that both may pass through a period of devaluation in which, technical facility having marched on and musical tastes having changed, they are believed to be perhaps less great than they were once considered. Andrés Segovia still fills concert halls in the last phase of his incredible career, but he too may eventually have his detractors. When they speak we should, however, never forget that, but for the work and influence of Segovia there would have been no platform (other than that of salon and coterie dimensions) for us to work on, no global world of the guitar for us to inhabit, and perhaps no pressing reason for this book to have been written. We are *all* standing on his shoulders.

JOHN W. DUARTE

London

*Andrés Segovia est et restera toujours "Le grand Seigneur" de la Musique dont il demeure le plus émouvant des grands interprètes. Son immense culture, son admirable ferveur ont fait de lui un grand exemple pour tous.*

*Je suis ému et fier de pouvoir exprimer en quelques mots mon affection, ma reconnaissance profonde pour l'inspiration qu' Andrés Segovia a su prodiguer à l'élite musicale du Monde entier par son style unique, par les admirables couleurs sans cesse renouvelées d'un jeu subtil, poétique, créateur d'un langage unique dans son raffinement, et toujours exprimé au seul service de la Musique.*

Andrés Segovia is, and always will be, the "grand seigneur" of music; of the great interpreters he remains the most moving. His immense culture, his admirable devotion have made him a great example for all of us.

I am touched and proud to be able to express in a few words my affection, my deep awareness of the inspiration which Andrés Segovia has lavished on the musical élite of the whole world by his unique style, his marvellous colours constantly changing in subtle and poetic performance. He is the creator of a language unique in its refinement and always expressed solely in the service of music.

PIERRE FOURNIER

Geneva

*Un concierto de Andrés Segovia es siempre una lección para todos los que nos dedicamos al arte. En su última actuación en Washington pasé a saludarle en su camerino en el intermedio. No se podía verle y estaba claro que algo ocurría. Dejé una nota pues al final tenía que ir a una recepción y no me era posible saludarlo. Antes de que pudiese marcharme, al saber quién era, me mandó llamar y charlamos un ratito. Resultó que se habia cortado en un dedo y sangraba. Además tocaba con una guitarra prestada, pues la suya se habia abierto con los cambios de temperatura y humedad. Nada se habia notado, ni se apreció después en el concierto. El éxito, inmenso, habia empezado dos meses antes al agotarse las entradas el dia que se pusieran en la venta. Su salida al podium, con esa dignidad que su gran figura impone, fué impresionante. Y luego su arte! Como si fuera el primer dia, dándolo todo, sabiendo que no se puede vivir de un nombre, por grande que sea. Me impresionó profundamente. Qué gran lección y cuánto podemos aprender de él. Con esa nobleza de "gentilhombre", hoy además consagrada por el título que la Monarquía española le ha concedido, explicó música de varios siglos, iluminandonos a todos. Gracias Maestro!*

A concert by Andrés Segovia is always a lesson to all of us who dedicate ourselves to art. At his last performance in Washington, I went to his dressing room to greet him during the interval. It was not possible to see him and it was clear something had happened. I left a note because I had to leave before the end to attend a reception and so would not be able to pay my respects. Before I had time to leave, when he found out who it was, he had me called back and we chatted for a while. It turned out that he had cut his finger and it was bleeding. Moreover he was playing a borrowed guitar, because his own had split with the changes in temperature and humidity. None of this showed, nor did it

25

later in the concert. The huge success had begun two months earlier when the tickets were sold out on the day they went on sale. His stage presence, with that dignity which his great figure commands, was impressive. And then his art! As though it were the first occasion, giving everything, knowing that he cannot live on his name alone no matter how great. He made a profound impression on me. What a great example and how much we can learn from him. With that nobleness of a gentleman, which is now further honoured by the title bestowed on him by the Spanish Monarchy, he presented the music of different centuries shedding light on us all.

Thank you, Maestro!

RAFAEL FRÜHBECK DE BURGOS

Madrid

It is given to few artists to transform the public's attitude towards their instrument; Andrés Segovia is one of this select band, and musicians salute him for his artistry, his generosity and his humanity. What his great compatriot Pablo Casals did for unaccompanied Bach is reflected in Segovia's contribution to the repertoire of the classical guitar.

SIR CHARLES GROVES

London

Spain had a Velázquez, a Cervantes, a Falla, and there is Andrés Segovia whose genius I have had the privilege to admire throughout the years. He set an example of true mastery of guitar playing, which hopefully, the next generations will follow.

IDA HAENDEL

London

26

*Den grossen Künstler und lieben Menschen Andrés Segovia grüsst an seinem Ehrentage in froher Erinnerung an harmonische Beisammensein im Zeichen der Musik mit herzlichen Wünschen für noch viele weitere Jahre in Gesundheit und Lebensfreude sein alter Freund*

Greetings to the great artist and dear person Andrés Segovia on his special birthday with happy memories of harmonious times together in the name of music. With heartfelt wishes for very many further years of health and zest for life from his old friend

WILHELM KEMPFF

Munich

Great artists of the kind of Andrés Segovia are very few and far between, and when one meets one of those torch-bearers of civilization it is like coming face to face with Nature's miracles created for the benefit of all mankind.

I only had the honour of meeting Maestro Segovia twice, once when, still as a young man, he took my then home town — Budapest — by storm, and much later, when I visited Spain. His playing electrified his audiences on each occasion; he made the guitar from an instrument of popular entertainment into a vehicle of serious classical music, thus inscribing his name in the annals of music history.

LOUIS KENTNER

London

In Andrés Segovia there dwells that quiet fire — fierce yet controlled — which is the mark of the Spaniard.

Where other peoples must rekindle their fires whilst yet others cannot govern them, the supreme artistry of a Segovia, of Casals, of Conchita Supervia, of Victoria de los

27

Angeles, or of Placido Domingo, is proof of an eternal flame
— inextinguishable because fed by every great civilization
and race which could cross the Mediterranean — diagonally,
lengthwise or crosswise — for thousands of years.

On Andrés Segovia's ninetieth birthday, may we thank
him for giving us the rhythm we need to carry on, the
melody we need to connect one day, one event, to the next,
the harmony we must have to remain in tune with our
fellow-dwellers and the serenity to distance ourselves in
time, space and thought.

YEHUDI MENUHIN

London

Paderewski was regarded as the king in his sphere in the
early 1900's, Casals was similarly exalted; today however the
standard of musicianship and virtuosity has reached a level
that it is now impossible to single out one artist above his
fellows and say "He alone is supreme". The exception
proves the rule.

Maestro Andrés Segovia's name is venerated not only for
his matchless playing, not only for the joy he has given us
but because he has led the way and created a new world of
music-making. His guitarist disciples inspired by him with
the highest aspirations are countless.

A happy birthday to Andrés Segovia. I join with everyone
the world over in sending my love to a great and good man,
to this most modest and lovable of artists.

GERALD MOORE

Buckinghamshire

My very best wishes to Andrés Segovia — certainly the
Maestro is responsible for bringing classical guitar "*al massimo*

28

*dello splendore"*, and is an artist I have always respected and admired tremendously.

LUCIANO PAVAROTTI

Modena

*De la severa personalidad de Andrés Segovia, quisiera señalar y resaltar tres facetas. La primera, naturalmente, su figura de guitarrista, capitán de aquel reducido pelotón de pioneros que lucharon devodadamente por sacar la guitarra de su reducido ámbito, de aquella especie de simpática masonería, que practicamente la tenia escondida, él supo lanzarla con fuerza irresistible allá por los años 20, al palenque instrumental.*

*La segunda faceta es la pedagogica, aunque la constante habilidad como virtuoso le haya impedido ejercer una continuada tarea en aquel sentido; no obstante y siempre con voluntad de apostolado, Segovia ha dedicado muchas horas de su que hacer guitarristico a la enseñanza ya crear una escuela que perpetúe su concepto y su manera de tocar la guitarra. Y la tercera de estas tres facetas, faceta inusitada entre los intérpretes, ha sido la promoción de su instrumento, invitando, instando, procurando que los músicos conocidos se acerquan y escriban para la guitarra, haciendoles amar este instrumento e incluso descubriendo nuevos valores y despertando en ellos el deseo de escribir para la guitarra.*

*Tengo la convicción de que estas tres virtudes entre otras forman la personalidad de este incomparable artista, figura historica de la guitarra.*

There are three facets in the strong personality of Andrés Segovia to point out and emphasize. The first of course, is his role as guitarist, leader of that small group of pioneers who struggled devotedly to extend the limited scope of the guitar; one of that devoted brotherhood who, when the instrument was practically unknown, hurled it with irresistible strength into the instrumental arena back in the '20s.

The second facet is that of the pedagogue; although his recognized accomplishment as a virtuoso prevented him

29

from following the task continuously in this direction, nevertheless with the enthusiasm of an apostle Segovia dedicated many hours of his guitar activities to teaching and in fact created a school to perpetuate his concept and style of playing the guitar.

And the third of these three facets, an unusual one among performers, has been the advancement of his instrument, inviting, urging, endeavouring to get well-known musicians to rally round and write for the guitar; making them love this instrument and thus discover new values, and awakening in them the desire to write for the guitar.

I am convinced that these three virtues, among others, form the personality of this incomparable artist, this historic figure of the guitar.

JOAQUÍN RODRIGO

Madrid

Andrés Segovia! A name which conjures up many images for me: a child entranced by the sounds of his guitar, a youngster awed by his overcoming the hitherto considered impossibilities of his instrument, a young man admiring his unbending principles toward his art, and his refusal toward the commercialization of his fame. Today, half a century later, all the above merges into a belief that as an artist and as a human being there is but one unique man in all the fields of interpretative art — Segovia.

JANOS STARKER

Indiana

Dear Friend and Colleague,
It is a particular privilege to join with your host of friends

around the world in saluting you on your ninetieth birthday.
You are a vibrant and living example of the wonderful remark
once made by George Bernard Shaw: "The greatest thing in
life is to die young — but delay it as long as possible." I know
of no one who has kept for so long his youthful vitality,
intellectual vigor and, most of all, joie de vivre. Your life-long
love affair with music is equalled only by the love that your
public, colleagues and friends in the concert halls all over the
world have for you in their hearts.
With great affection and respect,

ISAAC STERN

New York


I met Andrés Segovia in 1925 at a dinner given for him by
Henry Prunières, the director of the famous "La Revue
musicale", and a prominent figure in the international
musical life in between the two wars. The greatest
musicians, Parisians and foreigners, attended always the
Prunières evenings. Segovia, still unknown in Paris, played,
and I can hardly express my, and the general, enthusiasm
and unconditional admiration. I never could imagine that it
is possible to express on a guitar such musicianship, such
sense of style, such deep approach to the works, such
technical and colour possibilities.

I am proud to have been among the first composers to
have written a work for him (Mazurka in 1925–6). Since
then, I wrote many works for him, all recorded by him and
being part of his concert repertoire.

Segovia is my dearest friend, I consider him as a brother.

There is hardly a big city where we didn't meet — Paris,
London, Rome, Madrid, New York, Los Angeles, etc.

His musical genius, his enormous culture and his
generosity always fascinate me after almost sixty years of
uninterrupted friendship. I spent several vacations in his
wonderful Andalucian place; we visited together Seville,
Granada, Córdoba, and then, the return to Madrid. It was

31

unforgettable and Segovia's hospitality is undescribable.

The artist brings joy and contemplation all over the world. May he do so for many, many years, as wishes him his old and devoted friend

ALEXANDRE TANSMAN

Paris

I never thought when I was an adolescent in Paris that I would one day have the privilege to express in a book about Andrés Segovia my feelings about his artistry. But such a privilege is also a challenge for how can anyone express or explain what he is feeling when a miracle occurs?

I recall as a pure enchantment the recitals that I heard in Paris by this unique artist some fifty years ago and, between many many pearls, I shall never forget his record of Bach's Courante in C major.

Besides, shortly before she died, his friend, Mrs Tillett, told me that Andrés Segovia "has not cancelled one concert till now" which shows that the love the King of the guitarists has for people equals the one he has for his art.

PAUL TORTELIER

Nice

It is an honour and wholehearted pleasure to add my voice to this celebratory volume on the occasion of the ninetieth birthday of Andrés Segovia. By virtue of his extraordinary gifts of musicianship and technique, Segovia achieved and has maintained through his long lifetime a prime place in his chosen field of guitar performance. But above and beyond his stellar role as a performer, he has effected a major change in an area of music performance never before successfully fulfilled, namely, that which is now accepted as the world of the classical guitar. Seldom does a performing artist

32

influence the course of music history to the extent of creating a fresh musical field and direction for development by following generations of musicians throughout the world. This Segovia has done to a remarkably successful degree. Because of him, I now find myself seriously involved with the lute music of Johann Sebastian Bach — that is, more strictly speaking, music directly ascribed by Johann Sebastian, to the best of our present knowledge, and that which has been ascribed by others of his time, to the lute or lautenclavicymbal, Bach's own design for a lute-harpischord. My studies were done independently, but it is due to Segovia's development of the field for classical guitar that I have associated my work with this instrument, accepted a rarely talented guitarist as my student and as a result of almost five years of work have now made settings for an ongoing series of these works for publication.

Segovia perceived and fulfilled the concept of the classical guitar as an expressive and suitable medium for the performance of the greatest art, music, and this in turn led to proliferating directions of repertoire and contemporary composition for the instrument which has aroused international interest and created new concert-going audiences.

Thus Andrés Segovia has enriched the world with great achievements for which I, in my own work and appreciation, and all those who have benefited directly or indirectly by his artistic creativity and the glow of inspiration he has shed, must give thanks.

ROSALYN TURECK

Oxford


On behalf of the Council, Professors and Students of the Royal College of Music I have pleasure in sending affectionate greetings and good wishes on his ninetieth birthday to Andrés Segovia (Fellow of this College), one of the great musicians of this century, who has shared his remarkable gifts with countless music-lovers throughout the world.

SIR DAVID WILLCOCKS

The Director
Royal College of Music, London

I retain a vivid impression of the first time I heard Segovia in concert some fifty years ago in Madrid, at the "Teatro de la Comedia". One of the pieces he played was the Sonatina by Moreno Torroba and I was captivated by his rendition of the tone colour of his guitar.

Since then, our paths have crossed many, many times as friends and interpreters. The musical community is greatly indebted to him as the virtual "discoverer" of the guitar as a concert instrument. He continued in the tradition of Tárrega, but gave the guitar an entirely new dimension, enriched the repertoire, and most important, he can take pride in the loyalty of an immense public all over the world that succumbed to the charm of the guitar.

NICANOR ZABALETA

San Sebastian

To salute Maestro Andrés Segovia on his ninetieth birthday is to recognize not only his contribution to music in our century, but also the example that he has set us as an artist, both in his dedication to his art and in his humanity.

PINCHAS ZUKERMAN

34

# 3

# THE GUITAR IN ANDALUSIA

DURING THE years of Segovia's childhood in Andalusia, the presence of the guitar was an obvious feature of everyday life. Its status as a musical instrument to be taken seriously was entirely questionable, but the guitar's sound, as accompaniment to dance and song as well as for solo music, could be heard as a normal accepted part of Spanish life.

To the Spanish people this was a natural aspect of their cultural environment, but the steady stream of foreign travellers to this part of Spain responded rather differently, revelling in the vitality and spontaneous joie de vivre they found in streets and gardens. Many accounts of the experience of travellers from the nineteenth and early twentieth centuries can still be found and their writing provides a testimony to the background of Segovia's formative years as a child in an unspoiled region rich in its own cultural traditions.

Spain and the guitar have remained close companions for centuries. Other nations have been periodically fascinated by the instrument's appeal and throughout Europe at various times in history there have been intense bursts of guitar activity involving both performance and publication. But the Spanish speaking peoples have remained especially faithful to the guitar not only in Spain itself but in all those places where conquistadores or Spanish settlers carried their country's culture.

An English writer, L. Higgin, summed up Spanish musicality in the following way:

> Wherever two or three men and women of the lower classes are to be seen together in Spain during their playtime, there is a guitar, with short stanzas by unknown authors, many, perhaps, improvised at the moment. The *Jota,* the *Malagueña,* and the *Seguidilla* are combinations of music, song, and dance. . . . All are love-songs, most of them of great grace and beauty . . . throughout the length and breadth of Spain, outside the wayside *Venta* or the barber's shop, in the *patios* of

inns, or wherever holiday-makers congregate, there is the musician twanging his guitar, there are the dancers twirling about in obvious enjoyment, and to the accompaniment of the stamping, clapping, and encouraging cries of the onlookers, and the graceful little verse with its probably weird and plaintive cadence —

> Era tan dichoso antes
> De encontrarte en mi camino!
> Y, sin embargo, no siento
> El haberte conocido.

> I was so happy before
> I had met you on my way!
> And yet there is no regret
> That I have learned to know you.

(*Spanish Life in Town and Country,* London, 1902)

The guitar was clearly associated with spontaneous music-making, with song and dance. The three elements merged in a particular cultural blend involving poetry, music and movement. Another writer, Walter M. Gallichan, presents a similar picture in his description of Seville's *feria* of 1902:

One of the most interesting streets of the fair is that of the *casetas* or pavilions of the influential Sevillians, who spend the day in receiving guests, dancing, guitar playing and singing. The doors of the *casetas* are open. You can look within at the merry company. The old folk sit around on chairs: someone clicks a pair of castanets, and a graceful girl begins to dance. Fans are fluttering everywhere; there is a soft tinkling of guitars. . . .

(*The Story of Seville,* London, 1903)

In this account the Sevillians are not gypsy flamenco players but the *giorgio* (non-gypsy) citizens. For both gypsy and citizen of Seville the sound of the guitar was an ever present aspect of every-day life.

An earlier more famous tourist, Washington Irving, travelling through Andalusia in the spring of 1829 had made similar observations:

While we were supping with our drawcansir friend, we heard the notes of a guitar and the click of castanets, and presently a chorus of voices singing a popular air . . . the guitar passed from hand to hand but a

36

jovial shoe-maker was the Orpheus of the place. He was a pleasant-looking fellow, with huge black whiskers; his sleeves were rolled up to his elbows. He touched the guitar with masterly skill, and sang a little amorous ditty with an expressive leer at the women, with whom he was evidently a favourite.

*(Tales of the Alhambra)*

Later Irving identifies in a similar manner to L. Higgin, the delight the Spanish take in the guitar and its importance in their daily life:

Give a Spaniard the shade in summer and the sun in winter, a little bread, garlic, oil, and *garbances,* an old brown cloak and a guitar and let the world roll on as it pleases. Talk of poverty! with him it has no disgrace. It sits upon him with a grandiose style, like his ragged cloak. He is a *hidalgo,* even when in rags.

In a book published ten years before Segovia's birth, George Parsons Lathrop attempted to express the sense of inner dignity and the wit of the native Andalusian. Spain was portrayed in travel literature right up to the 1930s as a most foreign country and in publications around the turn of the twentieth century there are faint echoes of culture shock, partly stylized and partly genuine. During a trip to southern Spain Lathrop pursues anecdotes and atmosphere in a passage not too far distant from some of the stories related by Segovia himself.

An English lady conversing with a Sevillan gentleman who had been making some rather tall statements, asked him: "Are you telling me the truth?"

"Madam," he replied gravely, but with a twinkle in his eye, "I am an Andalusian!" At which the surrounding listeners, his fellow-countrymen, broke into an appreciative laugh.

So proverbial is the want of veracity, or to put it more genially, the imagination, of these Southerners. Their imagination will explain also the vogue of their brief, sometimes pathetic, yet never more than half-expressed, scraps of song, which are sung with so much feeling throughout the kingdom to crude barbaric airs, and loved alike by gentle and simple. . . . It is not a high nor a cultivated order of music, but there lurks in it something consonant with the broad, stimulating of the sun, the deep red earth, the thick strange-flavoured wine of the Peninsula. . . . Endless preludes and interminable windings-up enclose the minute kernel of actual song; but to both words and music is lent a repressed touching power and suggestiveness by repeating, as is always

37

done, the opening bars and first words at the end, and then breaking off in mid-strain. For instance:

> All the day I am happy,
> But at evening orison
> Like a millstone grows my heart.
> All the day I am happy. (Limitless Guitar Solo)

(Spanish Vistas, New York, 1883.)

The unity of poetry and music, and the strength of Andalusian culture are well evoked a few lines further on, again put in rhapsodic terms:

> Such evident ardour of feeling and such wealth of voice are breathed into these fragments that they become sufficient. The people supply from their imagination what is barely hinted in the lines. Under their impassive exteriors they preserve memories, associations, emotions of burning intensity, which throng to aid their enjoyment, as soon as the muffled strings begin to vibrate and syllables of love or sorrow are chanted.

In his autobiography, Segovia's description of his childhood bears witness to the accuracy of these travellers' impressions so far removed from the clamour of the modern age. Segovia's first memory is that of his uncle's rhyme accompanied by an imitation of playing the guitar:

> El tocar la guitarra
>   jum!
> no tiene 'cencia'
>   jum!
> sino fuerza en el brazo
>   jum!
> Permanecencia
>   jum!

"To play the guitar needs no science, only a strength in the arm and perseverance." Perhaps the belief that the guitar requires only perseverance and not too much knowledge is a belief still held among some Spanish people. Segovia remembered the actions accompanying the verse as "the first musical seed to be cast in my soul".

Not unsurprisingly, in an environment where the guitar was omnipresent, Segovia's first encounter with the instrument was when he heard the playing of a flamenco guitarist performing a

38

Generalife, the Summer Palace, Granada (c. 1907).

Moorish columns in the Alhambra (c. 1907).

Gypsies in Granada (c. 1907).

*soleares,* "which penetrated through every pore of my body". This player gave the young Andrés his first instructions on the guitar, a unique and touching historical moment even if the vagrant could teach him very little.

At the age of ten Segovia moved to Granada with his uncle and aunt. His childhood, in that time before radio and television, cars, aeroplanes, mass tourism, and the many encroachments on the individual's development imposed by contemporary living, is perhaps unimaginable to us today. The music of the guitar, snatches of Andalusian poetry, and folkloric culture were a natural part of his existence even if later he felt the need to transcend the limitations of provincial Spain.

Granada today is a thriving and busy city, frequently clogged with traffic, its Alhambra Palace and other historical monuments acting as a magnet for thousands of tourists each day. The spirit of calm present at the turn of the century can never be restored. Yet as early as 1908 the travel writer John Lomas was aware of the process of change:

> But even middle-aged Granada is fast passing away . . . the heights of the wonderful Sierra Nevada have been opened out to the tourist by funicular railway; while the up-to-date hotel enterprise is somewhat painfully *en evidence.*
>
> (*Spain,* London, 1908.)

Yet Granada has perhaps evolved two identities, in the same way as cities such as Paris or Jerusalem. On one level there is the physical appearance of the city, distinctive, yet containing many of the usual features of the twentieth century environment. But beyond that is an imaginative, symbolic, or spiritual presence, to which travellers and inhabitants still respond.

That spirit of place has been captured by several visitors at the end of the nineteenth century:

> There was one evening in Granada when we sat in a company of some two dozen people, and one after another of the ladies took her turn in singing to the guitar of a little girl, a musical prodigy. . . . Through the twanging of the strings we could hear the rush of water that gurgles all about the Alhambra.
>
> (George Parsons Lathrop, *Spanish Vistas.*)

It was this nostalgic aura of old Spain which the critic, Bernard Gavoty discerned at the heart of Segovia's interpretative style,

41

especially in his playing of pieces such as Albéniz's *Granada*:

He has bent down very low to listen to the voice of his well-beloved. She is telling him a long story, an old Andalusian legend: "It was in Granada I remember. There was there. . . ." . . . The sentence is left hanging, "like everything which is lovely on earth and which dies without uttering its final word." Where Segovia leaves the tale, the music takes it up, leading us in a dream to a place where human words cannot attain. What adjectives can ever bring Granada before us? But let those wise fingers be employed on the six taut strings: they will call up the chirping of the grasshopper, wing-shells rubbing together, the rasping saw of the cricket, the toad's golden blisters, the nocturnal fairyland of the slumbering gardens — and Granada, like a rose in the night, rises, swaying under the silvery moon.

(Bernard Gavoty, *Segovia,* Great Concert Artists, Geneva, 1955.)

Such romantic gestures may seem inappropriate in the headlong rush of New York, London, Madrid and Paris, yet Segovia as a child was deeply in touch with the unselfconscious serenity of old Andalusia and his playing, whether on record or in concert, is always a response to that distant experience. The harassed urban-ites all over the world who have faithfully attended Segovia's recitals over the last few decades have certainly shared and responded to these intimations of Eden. His own writing, passionately "old-fashioned" yet disturbingly relevant, like his playing, stirs echoes of that age of innocence and fantasy now lost somewhere in the twentieth century but not entirely forgotten:

Many were the hours I spent in my youth in dreamy meditation, hearing the murmurs of the streams of the Alhambra in harmony with the rustle of the old trees of El Bosque and the passionate song of the nightingale.

(*Andrés Segovia: an autobiography of the years 1893–1920,*
London/New York, 1976)

# 4

# THE FORMATIVE YEARS

ANDRÉS SEGOVIA was born in Linares, Jaén, in that region of Spain known as Andalusia on 21 February 1893. The significant details of his early childhood and upbringing are given in his autobiography, much of which was first published in serial form in the New York *Guitar Review* in 1947.

Unlike other more extrovert artists, Segovia has both in his book and in interviews preferred to concentrate on his musical career rather than on personal details. His favourite anecdotes mainly concern the furtherance of the guitar and its elevation to its present status as an accepted and popular concert instrument.

Segovia's life falls into various important developmental periods during that "steep climb to success" of which he often speaks when giving encouragement to young players. The unrelenting struggle to master the guitar, to extend the repertoire by direct appeal to composers, to transcribe and publish works of substance from many centuries, and to carry the guitar to the public throughout the world — in these activities he has never faltered. Yet the journey was undertaken step by step, and the beginning of the ascent, when the way forward was not always precise, was perhaps as tortuous as any part of the task.

The first stage of Segovia's career was accomplished at the Centro Artístico in Granada in 1909 when he gave his public debut at the age of sixteen. By this time, slowly and very much by his own efforts, Segovia had acquired a technique, a repertoire of a kind culled from various sources, and a good measure of that inner vision necessary to sustain his quest for the guitar's hidden identity. His grounding in music had involved a rejection, instinctive and final, of formally accepted instruments such as violin, 'cello or piano as far as personal study was concerned. But as time went on and he discovered friends who were competent players of such instruments, he learned certain principles from them that he applied to his own study of the guitar. Thus the young man concentrated all his faculties and enthusiasm on solving the problems of the guitar from an early age. As we have seen, the sound of the instrument was a daily feature of life in Andalusia, and Segovia was in touch with guitarists from his childhood onwards even if many of them were rough and unsophisticated performers.

In his teens Segovia deepened his knowledge of musical rudiments and of musical history and became familiar with the works of Bach, Mozart and Beethoven among others. He became aware of the nineteenth century virtuosi of the guitar including Sor, Aguado, Giuliani, Arcas and Tárrega, the High Priest of the Spanish guitar revival, whom Segovia was destined never to meet.

Francisco Tárrega (1852–1909), unlike most guitarists, had started as a pianist and this wider perspective enabled him not only to compose his own highly original works for the guitar but also to select and arrange suitable pieces by J.S. Bach, Handel, Haydn, Mozart, Beethoven, Paganini, Schubert, Berlioz, Mendelssohn, Chopin, Schumann, Wagner, and Grieg, etc. as well as Spanish works by Iradier, Arcas, Caballero, Chueca, Chapi, Albéniz, Calleja, Malats and Valverde. Through these transcriptions by Tárrega, Segovia achieved that dynamic fusion between the guitar and the broad mainstream of music which he so desired. At the same time he built up his technical ability with studies and pieces by Sor, Giuliani and Aguado, the guitarist's equivalent of piano pedagogues such as Clementi, Czerny, Joseffy and Hanon. Segovia's knowledge of theory was increased by the reading of *Método de Armonía* by Hilaríon Eslava (1807–1878), one of the leading nineteenth century composers of Spanish religious music.

According to Segovia's autobiography, his repertoire up to 1909 consisted mainly of such items as Sor's B minor Study Op. 35 No. 22, Tárrega's Capricho Arabe, Preludes and arpeggio Studies, as well as the latter's transcriptions of works by Bach, Beethoven, Mendelssohn, Chopin and Schumann. However, by the time of Segovia's recitals in Barcelona, Madrid and Granada from 1916 onwards, following a fruitful apprenticeship in Córdoba, Seville and Madrid, a more substantial series of programmes had evolved.

Interspersed with original guitar works from various composers including Napoleon Coste (1806–1883), Miguel Llobet (1878–1938), Tárrega, and Segovia himself (though some of these

44

Segovia, third from the left, listens to the playing of Miguel
Llobet. The group consists from left to right, standing:
Severino García Fortea, name unknown, Juan del Moral
Parras. Seated: a son of Francisco Tárrega, Andrés Segovia,
Miguel Llobet, another son of Tárrega.

pieces are now lost), were not only the Tárrega transcriptions but also the magnificent Llobet arrangements of compositions by Granados. Segovia had learned these pieces, which included such classics as La Maja de Goya (Tonadilla) and Danzas Españolas Nos. 5 and 10, direct from Llobet, a former pupil of Tárrega and at this stage fulfilling the role of mentor and exemplar to the young Segovia.

### Galerías Layetanas, Barcelona 28 January 1916

#### I

| | | |
|---|---|---|
| I | Song without Words | Mendelssohn |
| II | Melody<br>The Happy Peasant | Schumann |
| III | Waltz<br>Nocturne | Chopin |

#### II

| | | |
|---|---|---|
| I | Allegro in A | Coste |
| II | El Mestre | Llobet |
| III | Granada | Albéniz |
| IV | Capricho Arabe | Tárrega |

#### III

| | | |
|---|---|---|
| I | Andalucia | Segovia |
| II | La Maja de Goya | Granados |
| III | Spanish Dance in E | Granados |
| IV | Spanish Dance in G | Granados |

### Centro Artístico, Granada 17 June 1917

#### I

| | |
|---|---|
| Minuet in E | F. Sor |
| Tema con Variaciones | F. Sor |
| Serenata | J. Malats |

46

| | |
|---|---|
| *Scherzo — Gavotta* | F. Tárrega |
| *Capricho Arabe* | F. Tárrega |

## II

| | |
|---|---|
| Loure | J.S. Bach |
| First Movement from "Moonlight Sonata", Op. 27 No. 2 | L. van Beethoven |
| Berceuse | R. Schumann |
| Valse | F. Chopin |
| Nocturne | F. Chopin |

## III

| | |
|---|---|
| Lo Mestre | M. Llobet |
| L'hereu Riera | M. Llobet |
| Granada | I. Albéniz |
| Cadiz | I. Albéniz |
| Danza | E. Granados |

*Alhambra Palace Hotel, Granada 19 June 1917*

## I

| | |
|---|---|
| Minuet in A | F. Sor |
| Allegretto y Finale | F. Sor |
| Allegro in A | N. Coste |
| Estudio | F. Tárrega |

## II

| | |
|---|---|
| Bourrée | J.S. Bach |
| Andante from Sonata Pathétique, Op. 13 | L. van Beethoven |
| Au Soir, Op. 12 No. 1 | R. Schumann |

47

| | | |
|---|---|---|
| Song without Words | | F. Mendelssohn |
| Canzonetta | | F. Mendelssohn |

*III*

| | | |
|---|---|---|
| Allegro in A | | H. Vieuxtemps |
| Mazurka | | P. Tchaikowsky |
| Danza | | E. Granados |
| La Maja de Goya | | E. Granados |
| Sevilla | | I. Albéniz |

*Sala Mozart, Barcelona 15 November 1917*

*I*

| | | |
|---|---|---|
| I | Serenata | Malats |
| II | Estudio | Tárrega |
| III | Spanish Dance | Granados |
| IV | Sevilla | Albéniz |

*II*

| | | |
|---|---|---|
| I | Sonata<br>Andante — Allegro non troppo —<br>Andantino grazioso — Allegro | Sor |
| II | Estudio | Sor |

*III*

| | | |
|---|---|---|
| I | Minuet | Haydn |
| II | Andante | Beethoven |
| III | Berceuse | Schumann |
| IV | Canzonetta | Mendelssohn |
| V | Romance | Mendelssohn |

From this time onwards the expansion of the repertoire became one of Segovia's most ardent ambitions. He himself followed

The Puerta del Sol, Madrid (c. 1913).

The Plaza Mayor, Madrid (c. 1913).

Tárrega's precedent by seeking out suitable works to arrange; his earliest transcriptions included not only the unlikely material of Debussy's Second Arabesque which did not permanently endure, but also Albéniz's Asturias (Leyenda) from the Suite Española (originally written for the piano), a piece previously performed in a less effective arrangement by Severino García Fortea (c.1850–1931).

Even before his South American tour in 1920 — during which his son, Andrés, now a painter in Paris, was born in Buenos Aires — the next vital phase of Segovia's work had begun. He now succeeded in persuading non-guitarist composers to provide original works for the instrument, the first of the many being Federico Moreno Torroba (b. 1891). Segovia had been dissatisfied that the available repertoire was polarised between transcriptions of the music of the great composers and original guitar pieces by minor composers such as Sor, Giuliani, and even Tárrega.

> For we must be honest: Fernando Sor, the best, and perhaps the only guitar composer of his epoch, is, except for a few undeniably beautiful passages scattered through his larger works and concentrated in many of his smaller ones, tremendously garrulous, and his position in the history of the guitar is far more important than in the history of music itself. The guitar unfortunately has never had a Bach, a Mozart, a Haydn, a Beethoven, a Schumann, or a Brahms, in comparison with whom the figure of Sor might be accurately judged. As for Tárrega, more saint than musician, as I have said before, more artist than creator, his slight works are only the pleasant flowerings of a delicate talent. Within the compass of Hispanic music, it hardly need be said that he lacks the greatness of Pedrell, Albéniz, Granados, Falla.
>
> (Segovia in *Guitar Review* No. 7, 1948)

Even before his debut in Madrid about 1912, Segovia had nurtured secret thoughts about approaching the leading composers of Spain such as Joaquín Turina and Manuel de Falla, to "act as their guide through the labyrinth of the guitar's technique. . . . I convinced myself at that moment, that they would become firm believers in the guitar" (the Autobiography, pages 59–60). But at this early stage the moment was not yet appropriate. Many concerts and a great deal of preparatory work over the next decade would be necessary before the great advance was possible. Yet with the gradual spread of Segovia's prestige his approach to

51

distinguished composers began to bear fruit.

By the time of the next bright manifestation of Segovia's comet, the Paris debut of 1924, his desire to draw as many composers as possible within the guitar's gravitational orbit had become good news for them as well as for him. The glittering success of the Paris concert (attended by distinguished dignitaries from the musical world including Madame Debussy, Manuel de Falla, Albert Roussel, Joaquín Nin and others), was a signal to the world that there would be no going back. The superb technique, the interpretative magic, the sheer charisma of his playing — all were there, and composers had but to ask to be allowed to harness their imaginations to Segovia's rising star.

Drawing by Miguel del Pino y Sardá for a recital by Segovia in Madrid, 1920. (Photo by the author.)

Segovia in the 1920s.
(Photo: courtesy of the Radio Times Hulton Picture Library.)

Segovia in the 1930s.
(Photo: reprinted from *The Guitar and Mandolin* by
Philip Bone, courtesy of Schott & Co., London.)

Segovia in the 1940s. (From the record sleeve *Andrés Segovia* (HMV Treasury: HLM 7134), courtesy of EMI.)

Segovia in the 1950s.
(Photo: courtesy of Ibbs & Tillett.)

Segovia in the 1960s.
(Photo: courtesy of Ibbs & Tillett.)

Segovia in the 1970s.
(Photo: courtesy of Ibbs & Tillett.)

Segovia standing before his portrait (painted by Miguel del Pino) in his Madrid apartment, June 1982. (Photo by the author.)

# 5

# THE YEARS OF
# FULFILMENT

SEGOVIA'S quest for a repertoire and a public began among
Spanish composers and Spanish audiences, and from that well-
rooted origin stretched out to the whole world. Mention has
already been made of the work of Federico Moreno Torroba, the
first non-guitarist composer to offer his services to the young
recitalist. A further precedent was set by Manuel de Falla whose
Homenaje pour Le Tombeau de Debussy was unfortunately the
only piece that the great Spanish master wrote especially for the
guitar. Its prestige and influence on subsequent composers was
considerable despite its brevity.

Homenaje, though edited by Miguel Llobet and first performed
by Emilio Pujol in Paris on 2 December 1922, became a piece
closely identified with Segovia. On 7 December 1926, he gave the
work its English première at the Aeolian Hall, London, and
became the first of many guitarists to record it. J.B. Trend
writing in Manuel de Falla and Spanish Music (New York, 1929),
remarks that the piece is by "no means ordinary, conventional
guitar-music" and "represents an attempt to make the guitar
speak with the language of Falla".

The limitations of "ordinary, conventional guitar-music" were
at this time the very aspects composers and players wished to
avoid, in the process creating a distinctive vocabulary for both the
guitar and those who wrote for it. The way forward at first could
only be gradual, relying on those precedents established by
twentieth century composers and, if possible, eschewing the early
prototypes of Sor, Aguado and Tárrega. In this way Torroba and
Falla began the process of extending the guitar's capabilities which
ensured that henceforth composers approached the instrument
with clear imaginations, liberated from clichés of the past. The
creative energies unleashed in this way influenced later generations
of musicians. Segovia's role as a midwife to the Muse was later
emulated by many other guitarists. The movement towards

bringing into existence a beautiful repertoire, undertaken at first rather tentatively and with no wide horizons visible, broadened into a remarkable deluge of works of many styles, nationalities and periods.

In the 1920s the foundations of this movement were well and truly achieved. Segovia's ever increasing circle of contacts among the world of composers continued to be impressed by the quality of his recitals and those items of repertoire previously coaxed from their colleagues. Each composition created and performed gave further evidence of the rich resources yet to be exploited.

Torroba's first guitar pieces, such as Danza in E from the Suite Castellana, were composed before 1920. Falla's Homenaje was brought into being about 1920–21, Joaquín Turina's Sevillana, was composed in 1923, and premièred by Segovia on 17 December of that year at the Madrid Society of Musical Culture. It was also in 1923 that Segovia met Manuel Ponce, Mexico's foremost composer, who began his life-long devotion to Segovia's guitar with a Sonata Mexicana in four movements, composed shortly after that first meeting.

It seems likely, though it is difficult to verify, that Segovia's debut in Paris on 7 April 1924, in the presence of Dukas, Falla, Madame Debussy, Roussel, Joaquín Nin, Miguel de Unamuno and others, included several of the above works, as well as the transcriptions of works by Albéniz and Granados. In the same year Segovia made debuts in Berlin and London, and a second tour of South America, including Argentina, Cuba (where he experienced his first recording session) and Mexico. Also during 1924 Segovia met a young American named George C. Krick in Munich, who later helped persuade Sol Hurok, the great impresario, to book Segovia for the USA. Altogether 1924 proved to be a vital year in the fortunes of both Segovia's career and the history of the guitar.

One immediate result of the Paris debut was a fine new work by the French composer, Albert Roussel (1869–1937). Segovia, Op. 29, was first performed in Madrid on 25 April 1925, and given its Paris première on 13 May of that year. The following month saw the appearance of Turina's little masterpiece Fandanguillo, Op. 36, completed on 4 June after a fairly rapid process of composition.

Also in 1925 came a significant first meeting with the Polish composer, Alexandre Tansman, who had settled in Paris. The result of their friendship was the publication in 1928 of a Mazurka, a work written (1925–26) as an immediate response to Segovia's masterly playing. The collaboration endured through the decades and was rewarded in 1951, when Tansman's Cavatina was awarded first prize at the Academia Chigiana's international composers' competition. Tansman's other suite, In Modo Polonico (Eschig, 1968) became from the 1950s onward, whether played complete or in part, a favourite of Segovia's recitals. Thus the friendships of the 1920s brought about long-term creative benefits.

In the same year, the French composer, Gustave Samazeuilh, wrote a most Spanish sounding Sérénade (Durand 1926). Samazeuilh, a pupil of Chausson, d'Indy and Dukas, had written works for the violinist Eugène Ysaÿe, as well as for the violin-piano duo of Jacques Thibaud and Alfred Cortot. His little Sérénade, though not frequently performed in the interim, weathered the storms of time to be finally immortalized in a Segovia recording as late as 1976.

On 2 March 1926, two years after the death of Lenin, Segovia encountered his first Russian audience, the recital being held in the hall of the Moscow Conservatory. This was the first major guitar concert by a foreign artist visiting Russia since Fernando Sor had played at the court of the Tsar following his arrival in Moscow in November, 1823. Segovia's debut took place in the year that Trotsky was expelled from the Politburo, and one year before the tenth anniversary of the Red Revolution.

Torroba's Fandanguillo, Arada and Danza, were published in 1926, among the first editions of Schott's Segovia Guitar Archive Series, as was Turina's Fandanguillo, Op. 36. This series was one of the most important publishing events in the guitar's history. At first, sales were sparse but in time to come the financial returns would be remarkable as works from the series began to be studied in academies by all students of the guitar and recitalists played them many times in concert. Recording royalties alone would ultimately prove phenomenal. Torroba's Burgalesa, Preludio, and Serenata Burlesca followed into print in 1928 and the ever popular Pièces caractéristiques appeared in 1931.

Another area of exploration arrived in the 1920s with the publication of J.S. Bach's lute works, edited by Dr Hans Dagobert

Bruger. *Johann Sebastian Bach, Kompositionen für die Laute,* (Möseler Verlag, Wolfenbüttel and Zürich) had reached a third edition by 1925, having been first published in 1921. During a trip to Germany Segovia discovered this volume and immediately began work on various pieces which were to become a familiar aspect of his recitals. Interviewed on the "Woman's Hour" programme on BBC radio in 1981, Segovia discussed his first encounter with Bruger's edition and exclaimed, "I was in Heaven when I discovered that!"

In 1928 a number of compositions of J.S. Bach were published in the Segovia Guitar Archives Series, including the little Prelude in C minor (arr. in D minor for guitar) BWV 999, the Allemande from the First Lute Suite, BWV 996, the Gavotte from the Fourth Lute Suite (BWV 1006a) and the Courante from the Third 'Cello Suite, among others. But the ultimate attempt to bring the sacred citadel of J.S. Bach within the guitar's territory was yet to come; Segovia's edition of the Chaconne, from the Partita No. 2 in D minor for unaccompanied violin, was published in 1934.

That some musicians regarded the transference of such a piece from its natural habitat of the violin repertoire to the unknown resonances of the guitar as a kind of blasphemy can hardly be doubted. For a recital in Paris on 4 June 1935, when the Chaconne was to be played for the first time in the French capital, Segovia asked Marc Pincherle to support his advocacy of Bach in suitably worded programme notes. Pincherle undertook this task, pointing out that not only does the Chaconne often give a "sense of discomfort" when played on the four strings of the violin, but also that Bach himself often "modified the destination of his works — changing an adagio in legato style from violin to harpischord, transferring a prelude for solo violin to an organ accompanied by orchestra."

Pincherle then evokes the name of Dr Bruger to reveal Bach's "devoted particular attention" to the lute. After this he rather jeopardizes the substance of his case by suggesting that Bach himself might have seen the Chaconne as having some connection with both the guitar and Andalusian music. The key of D minor, the harmonic progressions, and the Iberian origin of the Chaconne form, imply to Pincherle an admittedly frail hypothesis that the Chaconne was composed originally for a plucked instrument.

This slight degree of special pleading was perhaps a necessasry inducement to the audience to give Segovia a fair hearing at least.

This was achieved and Segovia joined the exclusive pantheon of musicians such as Ferruccio Busoni and Leopold Stokowski who have brought the most famous Chaconne in history to people's ears through other timbres than that known to J.S. Bach. From that time onwards the Chaconne became one of the Everests of the guitar's repertoire and all aspirants to honours would have to conquer it before their credentials could be fully acknowledged.

Around 1927 a new chapter in the guitar's history opened when Segovia's first recordings for HMV were issued. The pieces chosen for the first adventure in recorded sound included works by Federico Moreno Torroba, the Courante by J.S. Bach from the Third Lute Suite, Tárrega's Recuerdos de la Alhambra, the Serenata Española by Malats, and some compositions in baroque style by Manuel Ponce disguised under the name of the eighteenth century lutenist, Sylvius Leopold Weiss. Turina's Fandanguillo, Op. 36, also received the accolade of its first recording about this time.

On 29 April 1927, Segovia made his debut in Denmark; the review of this concert is included at the end of the chapter, "Images of Segovia". Throughout these years, as the repertoire accumulated, country after country fell under Segovia's spell and his experience of the musical responses of many nations increased.

In 1928 Segovia took on the most crucial tour of all, his first recitals in the United States. The story of his debut here was related in *Reader's Digest* of October, 1972:

> One reason for Segovia's insistence upon absolute silence is that the notes of a guitar are more susceptible to being drowned out than those of most other concert instruments. . . . For this reason he early learned to avoid giving recitals in private houses, as hostesses frequently invited too many guests and then proved incapable of keeping them quiet.
>
> On arriving in the United States for the first time in 1928, Segovia was annoyed to find that the first engagement for which he was booked was in a private house in the remote village of Proctor, Vermont. The mildest of men about everything except his devotion to the guitar, he threatened to cancel his tour unless he could be excused, and was only persuaded to reconsider on threats of serious legal penalties.
>
> When he reached the modest house in Proctor where he was to stay, Segovia was given supper and then shown to his room. He put on his evening clothes and at the appointed hour came downstairs in his

overcoat, grimly prepared to go wherever the concert was to be held. Only then did he learn that the concert was being held in the cottage where he was staying. Shown into the sitting-room, Segovia discovered that his entire audience consisted of three people: his elderly hostess, her companion and her brother.

The hostess explained that she had attended his debut in Paris and instantly become such an admirer that she had insisted on contracting for his first appearance in the United States, at the fee he normally received for playing to an entire concert hall. Deeply touched by this compliment, Segovia found playing for them one of the happiest evenings of his musical life.

Following this experience Segovia resumed his normal concert activities, appearing at the New York Town Hall for the first guitar recital in the city's history. Five sell-out concerts there were followed by a tour of forty other American venues in eleven weeks. Segovia's career in the United States was thus triumphantly launched, and later in the same year he made his debut in the Far East.

As we have seen, 1928 was the year when various works by J.S. Bach were published in Segovia's editions. The same year was the occasion for the publishing of several new works by Manuel Ponce, including his Thème Varié et Finale, Sonata III, Tres Canciones Populares Mexicanas, and Preludio, whilst Sonata Clásica (Hommage à Fernando Sor) and Sonata Romántica (Hommage à Schubert) appeared in print the following year. His twelve Preludes were issued in 1930, followed two years later by Variations on Folia de España and Fugue, the latter being recorded on 78 rpm's about this time.

In 1929 Segovia made his first visit to Japan, the precursor of many trips to a country which at the present time has thousands of students of the classical guitar including some world-class players and luthiers. Also in 1929 Segovia met Joaquín Rodrigo for the first time during a visit to Paris. During this year Heitor Villa-Lobos composed his Douze Études (Eschig, 1953), and dedicated them to Segovia. They are the most renowned set of guitar studies and a landmark in the repertoire, though performance in public of the complete set would fall to later generations.

Although 1929 saw the famous "Black Friday" of 28 October, when the New York Stock Exchange collapsed, Segovia's career forged ahead; in one decade he had gone from obscurity to international esteem, even if the best was yet to come.

The 1930's brought new and exciting developments. In 1932 Segovia travelled, after a strenuous series of recitals, to Venice and Provence with Manuel de Falla and Dr José Segura, a professor from the University of Granada. In Venice, Falla conducted *The Puppet Show* at the International Festival of Music. On their return Falla was not well, with the misfortune of having contracted an infection. The event is well described by Jaime Pahissa:

> They returned in Segovia's car. Falla had a very unpleasant boil on his right temple, which he attributed to an infection contracted from having shaken hands with so many people who came to congratulate him and which he had transferred to his forehead when putting on his glasses. In fact the condition affected his whole face and threatened to become very serious. On reaching San Remo, they had to stop to find a doctor. They were dressed in dusty travelling clothes, Segovia with long, unkempt hair, Falla with his face distorted by the swelling and pain. His friend Dr Segura was at least dressed with a tidiness which contrasted with the disorder of his companions. They went into the doctor's house, and Segovia introduced Falla with suitable eulogies as "the great composer, Manuel de Falla", and Falla likewise introduced the great guitarist with similar praise. The doctor regarded them distrustfully, as though he feared that they were lunatics. Then they introduced Dr Segura, who presented a more correct appearance. "Here's a more likely-looking person," exclaimed the doctor, shaking hands with him. The upshot was that he treated Falla very successfully, so that by the same afternoon they were able to continue their journey to Arles.
>
> (*Manuel de Falla, His Life and Works*, London, 1954.)

The visit to Venice, despite its somewhat chaotic aftermath, itself affected the history of the guitar. While at the International Festival Segovia met Mario Castelnuovo-Tedesco, one of the foremost Italian composers. The result was a creative fusion of interests which endured until Castelnuovo-Tedesco's death in 1968. The first work to be produced Variazioni (attraverso i secoli) was written shortly after the Festival, followed by the Sonata in D (Omaggio a Boccherini) Op. 77, (Schott, 1935), destined to become one of the high points of the Segovian repertoire. Other products of the 1930's by this prolific devotee of the guitar included Capriccio Diabolico, Op. 85, and Tarantella,

67

Op. 87a (both written in 1935 and published by Ricordi in 1939), and the Guitar Concerto in D, Op. 99, written in 1939 and premiered by Segovia in Montevideo that year, to be recorded in July 1949. Castelnuovo-Tedesco's Guitar Concerto also encouraged Manuel Ponce to complete his Concierto del Sur for guitar and orchestra, also receiving a first performance in Montevideo in October, 1941.

The establishment of a concerto repertoire for the guitar was another significant step forward. Though a few works for guitar and string orchestra had been written in the early nineteenth century by composers such as Giuliani and Carulli, the genre did not receive much further attention until the 1930s. Moreover composers such as Castelnuovo-Tedesco and Ponce, Rodrigo and Villa-Lobos (whose Concerto for guitar and small orchestra Segovia premiered with the Houston Symphony orchestra in 1959) were fascinated by the prospect of matching many orchestral colours with guitar timbres and did not restrict themselves to the former mixture of guitar and strings. Brass, woodwind, and percussion were now introduced to provide the guitar with imaginative and delicately orchestrated concertos. Before long these concertos became an integral part of the repertoire, popular with both audience and players, and since that time well over thirty concertos have been written, though the contributions of the four composers mentioned above have proved the most widely played.

In 1950 Castelnuovo-Tedesco produced yet another distinguished work, the Guitar Quintet, Op. 143, one of the few collaborations between guitar and string quartet to have been attempted by Segovia's circle of composers. Tonadilla on the name of Andrés Segovia of 1954 (Schott, 1956) is an example of Castelnuovo - Tedesco's graceful habit of offering musical greetings cards to guitarists, a kindness he extended in later years to several younger players as well as to Segovia.

In 1960 the Italian composer wrote twenty-eight pieces to accompany passages narrated from Juan Ramón Jiménez's prose-poem *Platero y Yo*. Segovia's recording of ten movements of these, without narrator, evokes some of the guitar's most sensuous and nostalgic sonorities. Thus a chance encounter of the 1930s produced lasting pieces for the repertoire, which have now endured for nearly four decades.

In 1936, at the beginning of the Civil War, Segovia was forced to leave Spain. Shortly after his departure his home in Barcelona was ransacked and looted, and many of his possessions and souvenirs of tours ended up in the street markets. He did not return for sixteen years. This absence may account for the fact that one of Spain's leading composers, Joaquín Rodrigo, did not find himself able to dedicate his famous Concierto de Aranjuez to Segovia. Rodrigo's biographer, Vicente Vayá Pla, makes it clear how the Spanish Civil War, trouble in Europe and Segovia's sojourn in Montevideo, made it impossible for Segovia to be offered the première of the work.

> It was never further from reality, during the years 1938 and 1939 — separated by oceans, by a war in Spain, with a world war in the offing — in fact it was totally impossible that Segovia would be able to give the first performance of this Concerto.
>
> (*Joaquín Rodrigo, Su Vida y Su Obra,* Madrid, 1977.)

However this apparent setback in the guitar's progress, depriving us of ever hearing Segovia perform this Concerto, was resolved in 1954 when Rodrigo composed Fantasia para un Gentilhombre, for guitar and orchestra. In this work the gentleman of the guitar, Segovia, is united in guitar history with the themes of Gaspar Sanz, the great Spanish guitarist of the seventeenth century, in a delicately inspired work of twentieth century lyricism.

Segovia later recorded Zarabanda Lejana, originally composed by Rodrigo for piano solo in 1926, as a homage to Luis Milán, the sixteenth century vihuela maestro. This composition was also orchestrated in a 1928 version, a Villancico being added to make up a diptych.

In 1963, the Guitar Archives edition published Rodrigo's Tres Piezas Españolas, (Fandango, Passacaglia and Zapateado). Segovia's recording and performance of the Fandango established the presence of another technical and interpretative pinnacle of the Spanish guitar repertoire, and was issued on the Golden Jubilee Album of 1959 to commemorate Segovia's fifty years of recitals since his Granada debut in 1909.

In the 1940's, during which Segovia took up residence in Montevideo, two big events determined the course of guitar history. The first of these was the introduction of nylon strings by Albert Augustine, a development which ended the age-old tradi-

69

tion of gut strings which were both melodious and unreliable. The second was the invention of the long-playing record. Technological advance of both kinds was eagerly sought by Segovia and he embraced these manifestations of progress with characteristic fervour.

The recordings of the 1950's, following his first long-playing records in 1947, represent some of the finest Segovia vintage. (They were a potent influence on the generation of guitarists destined to come into prominence in the 1960's such as Julian Bream and John Williams.) During these years, in his position as unrivalled maestro of the guitar, Segovia's presence was both an inspiration and a challenge to the younger pretenders to the throne. The fine harvest of the early years of persuading and cajoling composers of quality to write for the instrument, as well as the long labours of transcription and arrangement, stretched out at length to greet those who wished to follow in Segovia's path. Unlike Segovia's own youth, when the course to follow was imprecise, guitarists now had a greatly enlarged repertoire and a clearer idea of its scope and depth.

Following his seventieth birthday in 1963, Segovia continued full of vigour to dominate the guitar scene, giving recitals world-wide, inspiring composers, teaching at the Summer School in Siena established in the mid 1950's, recording many albums, and finding time to marry again and father another child. Despite family tragedies and cataract operations on his eyes Segovia's determination to take the guitar and its music to the public never wavered.

Various new works entered the repertoire. These included English Suite by John W. Darte, (recorded 1967, Novello 1967), written to commemorate Segovia's wedding, Federico Monpou's Suite Compostelana (Éditions Salabert, 1964), J. Munoz Molleda's Variations and Fugue on a Theme of Handel (Schott, 1970), all of which were recorded in the 1960's and were included in many recitals.

In the year before his ninetieth birthday, Andrés Segovia has undertaken several tours, including recitals in Japan and the United Kingdom. He has the further satisfaction of knowing that his pioneering example of giving recitals and encouraging composers has become part of the international guitarist's routine. Julian Bream, Alirio Diaz and John Williams, the three greatest exponents of the Segovia tradition, have similarly encouraged composers and had many works dedicated to them, and have continued to perform the masterpieces of Segovia's early years.

In a review of a recital given by Segovia in Chicago in 1980, Robert C. Marsh, wrote the following words; they express the profound devotion Segovia's artistry has inspired:

> So we had the exchanges of love that made the encores so rewarding. He came back and played for us again, was inundated with applause, returned without the instrument, heard even more applause, gestured gratefully that enough was enough, but as the applause went on, left the stage, returned with the guitar, and like a loving great grandfather, reciprocated and played yet again.
>
> The music was welcome, of course. The Spanish pieces that made up the encore group contained some of his most sensitive work of the evening. But there was more to it, holding back the clock and putting off, as long as possible, the moment of parting. For as we are always happy to welcome Segovia so too there is always a poignant moment when we say farewell. We never want to say farewell to this man. We want him with us, every year, forever.
>
> (*Chicago Sun-Times*, 20 February 1980.)

# 6

# SEGOVIA AND THE CONCERT HALL

> The guitar is like an orchestra, distant and mysterious, its sound coming to us as if from a world much smaller and subtler than ours.
> Andrés Segovia

SEGOVIA'S contribution to music since his debut in Granada in 1909 has been founded on his view of the guitar as an exquisite miniature orchestra. Armed with this vision, he has become the most celebrated and honoured guitarist the world has ever known. His career as an active recitalist has also been one of the most extended as, right up to his ninetieth year, he has followed his well established routine of international concert tours.

Segovia was the first guitarist to play regularly in large recital halls. Most leading players of the early twentieth century regarded the instrument as being best suited for the salon or drawing room, that intimate *ambiente* which for many generations had been the guitar's natural habitat. Segovia wished to extend the guitar's influence beyond a privileged élite of society into the same environment favoured by pianists or violinists of renown. Before Segovia, the guitarist could find no place in the mainstream of musical life, being destined to languish in quiet mediocrity among a coterie of his own persuasion or playing for a few well-informed patrons, devotees, pupils and camp-followers.

This necessary transference from the salon to the concert hall, developed from Segovia's early experience of giving recitals. Opposition to the move came from many sources, yet the success of the project and the performance of recitals in halls seating a thousand or more people was achieved quite soon in Segovia's career. The vital experiment was conducted at the Palau in Barcelona (about 1918). Segovia's autobiography emphasises that this step was a watershed in his progress:

If my concert at the Sala Granados was to be of great significance in my personal life, the last one I gave in Catalonia at that period played an important part in the history of the guitar as a concert instrument, something which in turn influenced my career.

I have already mentioned Llobet's categorical opinion regarding the guitar's "inability" to produce enough sound volume to be heard throughout large concert halls. This had also been said by Tárrega and his students. If they, the top exponents of the classical guitar, held such views, who could blame critics, audiences and other musicians for agreeing with them?

(*Andrés Segovia: an autobiography of the years 1893–1920*, p. 119)

Even today the guitar enjoys a double life. The existence of numerous Guitar Societies throughout the world provides a sanctuary where lovers of the instrument can hear recitals and discuss the finer points of technique and repertoire. The origins of these Societies go back to the nineteenth century when soirées organized by teachers of instruments, or gatherings in intimate surroundings of like-minded people, could provide an inexpensive and congenial setting for music of many kinds.

This double life, the division between private gatherings and public concerts, was also found in other spheres of music. In the first half of the nineteenth century some great pianists, including Chopin, preferred to frequent the salon rather than the concert hall. The pianist Alfred Cortot (whom Segovia heard in Córdoba about 1912, and whose playing he described as being "my first religious experience with music") explored the paradox of Chopin's pianistic fame:

> The light of fame illumines the name of no other pianist with greater brilliance than that of Chopin — an almost legendary brilliance, that even to this day is associated with the quite exceptional nature of his playing, and this quite independently of his genius as a composer.
>
> Paradoxically it is almost impossible to mention a virtuoso who had less contact with the public during the course of a professional career destined for immortality. Thirty concerts, the greater number of which were given without any sort of monetary reward and in no way enhanced his reputation as an artist (indeed, they were often no more than a casual appearance at a charity show) — these make up the sum total of his career as a soloist before the general public.
>
> (*In Search of Chopin*, London 1951.)

The same point is pursued, with interesting statistics, by a more recent writer:

73

The factual details of the background of Chopin's career are not to be disputed. His legendary reputation as a pianist was, for his whole life, based on a mere thirty or so genuinely *public* appearances. (One thinks of the scores of times a modern virtuoso may appear in a single year.) Very few were those who had heard Chopin play. His largest single audience was one of twelve hundred at a concert in Manchester, and not more than about six hundred persons, mostly aristocratic music-lovers, heard him during the last ten years of his life in France.

(Arthur Hedley, *Frédéric Chopin, Profiles of the Man and the Musician* ed. Alan Walker, London, 1966)

It was perhaps partly because of the intimacy and elegance of Chopin's career, as well as his fastidious artistry, that he became a potent musical exemplar for a guitarist such as Tárrega, whose mazurkas and polkas bear witness to a distant Polish spirit infusing the classical guitar.

Chopin's reticence in performance was perhaps due mainly to his nervousness on such occasions, described by Cortot as "a kind of pathological inhibition", as well as being "bound up with his slender reserves of bodily endurance". Chopin himself remarked:

I am not the right person to give concerts. The public intimidates me. I feel asphyxiated by the breath of people in the audience, paralysed by their curious stares and dumb before that sea of unknown faces.

If Chopin, transcendent genius that he was, considered himself psychologically unsuited for public concerts, such caution did not bother Liszt, to whom the above comments were addressed. Liszt, greatly impressed by Paganini's showmanship and large-scale presentation, was one of the first artists to use the term "recital". The word was probably suggested to him by Frederick Beale of the music firm of Cramer, Beale and Addison, a fact recorded by Thomas Willert Beale in *The Enterprising Impresario* of 1867. It was given out that M. Liszt "will give Recitals on the Pianoforte of the following works . . .". From 1850 onwards Hallé's "Pianoforte Recitals" became popular in Britain, appropriately for it was in London that Liszt first used the term.

As the concept of the "recital" gained ground, rampant virtuosity was often the order of the day. Many of those in the public eye were composer-performers who wrote dazzling works to impress the public with sheer pyrotechnics. This too changed:

74

Music, rather than stunts, began to be the thing. Interpreters started coming along who took the word "interpret" seriously, confining themselves to the music of the masters. A new species began to appear — the performing musician who was not necessarily a composer. These, aided as they were by concert halls rather than salons, helped the concert as an institution come into being. By the 1860s the battle put up by this new breed was virtually won, and concert programmes began to appear pretty much as they appear today.

(Harold C. Schonberg, *The Great Pianists*, London, 1964)

Schonberg also records two vital innovations, today accepted as commonplace, which assisted in the development of the recital structure as we now know it:

Although Liszt had been the first to give unaided solo recitals, it was Clara (Wieck-Schumann) who even more than Liszt broke the eighteenth-century format. Up to about 1835 the artist generally had to engage an orchestra, was expected to play his own music with it, had to arrange for guest artists to share the programme, and to vary his programme with short pieces, had to end with an improvisation. But by 1835 Clara was, for the most part, playing with just a few assisting artists, and moreover presenting nothing but the best. Mendelssohn had paved the way. In Berlin, on November 9 and December 1, 1832, he had played Beethoven's *Waldstein* and the E flat Sonata (Op. 27, No. 1) both apparently the very first time that these two sonatas had ever been played in public. When Clara played the complete *Appassionata* in Berlin in 1837, it was the first time it had been heard there, as far as anybody can ascertain. What is more, she played from memory. Leschetitzky maintained that she was the first pianist in history to do so. For this she was called, in some circles, "insufferable". Up through the 1840's it was held that to perform the work of a master without the notes was bad form: it showed disrespect to his art.

(*The Great Pianists*, pp. 225, 226.)

From this time onwards the conventions of recitals — performing complete works and playing from memory — became paramount. Yet many of these essential aspects of musical history were being formulated only half a century before Segovia's birth.

The movement from the salon to the concert hall whether it concerned Segovia or his virtuoso predecessors on other instruments, involved basic changes in approach. The friendly and informal mood of the small gathering with its more light-hearted approach, reflected in both repertoire and its presentation, now became only the occasional activity of the professional recitalist. The salon or intimate concert was based primarily on making contacts with patrons and hostesses whose own social kudos was maintained both by the quality of the artist invited to entertain the guests and by the position in society of those requested to attend.

Large concert halls were more democratic in that it was sufficient to buy a ticket to gain entrance, and tickets were not the prerogative of a chosen few. Concerts also became more impersonal and the figure of the impresario assumed a great significance in the lives of recitalists. At the same time the artist became more aloof from his public as he experienced the heady delights of playing to over a thousand people instead of a few dozen. From now on reputations in particular cities could be made on the grand scale almost overnight, followed by sponsorship throughout entire countries by the powerful impresarios.

Until Segovia's triumph at the Palau, guitarists had not thought it possible to enter the recital circuit in the same way as pianists or violinists, and while guitarists such as Tárrega had toured several countries, the expeditions were more limited than those undertaken by other instrumentalists, especially as the lack of concertos closed off one potentially profitable avenue. Segovia not only made people acknowledge that the big hall was a suitable venue for guitarists; he persuaded impresarios that they could make money out of hitherto unexplored areas of music.

By the time Segovia departed on his first trip to South America on the SS Queen Victoria in 1920, he was associated with the same impresario with whom Arthur Rubinstein had set sail for South America in May, 1917. Rubinstein explains in his autobiography how Quesada was engaged:

> With all my great success the Philharmonic Societies paid such small fees, and so did the Teatro Lara, that I really needed a good agent. A musician of my acquaintance told me about a man named Daniel, who used to work in Berlin in the office of the great Hermann Wolff, and I made an appointment with him for the next morning.
>
> I discovered that he was a Cuban — his real name was Ernesto de Quesada — and that he had inherited or bought a small printing firm named Daniel, a name which he kept for his concert agency. There was a boyish look about him, belying his thirty or more years, and he was rather shy, but I felt right away that he was the man I needed, a really competent concert agent.

76

"We can make much more money next season, but it takes some bargaining with the stingy Philharmonic Societies," he said. "In Madrid and Barcelona you ought to give your concerts at your own risk; after expenses the money is yours."

I engaged him as my agent for Spain — and he is still my representative today.

(Arthur Rubinstein, *My Young Years*, London 1973.)

Quesada required that Segovia, before being accepted on the agency's list, should first have a trial concert in Madrid, the previous debut at the Ateneo not being considered adequate as it had occurred some years before. The way was eased for Segovia by the 'cellist Gaspar Cassadó who, at first rebuffed by Quesada at the mention of the word "guitar", was later allowed to put up the money for the auditional recital, an experiment to be undertaken without a fee for Segovia. This concert took place at the ballroom of the Ritz Hotel. The reviews and the audience of over two hundred were favourable, and Quesada, who was tone-deaf but "had a fine sense of smell when it came to profits" offered Segovia a "multi-year exclusive contract".

*Hotel Ritz, Madrid 27 March 1917*
*I*

| | |
|---|---|
| Minuet | Sor |
| Rondo | |
| Theme and Variations | |
| | |
| Scherzo Gavotte | Tárrega |
| Capricho Arabe | |

*II*

| | |
|---|---|
| Loure | Bach |
| Berceuse | Schumann |
| Canzonetta | Mendelssohn |
| Romance | |
| Waltz | Chopin |

*III*

| | |
|---|---|
| Allegro in A | Coste |
| Granada | Albéniz |
| Cadiz | |
| Spanish Dance | Granados |

Until Quesada's retirement in 1956, his association with Segovia remained firm, a triumph for all concerned and for the future well-being of the guitar itself. For both Rubinstein and Segovia the collaboration with Quesada resulted in immediate tours of Spain and subsequent visits to Latin America. (Quesada's alliance with Rubinstein proved a significant step forward for Spanish music as the pianist soon became friendly with Manuel de Falla and the widow of Albéniz, and began to incorporate Iberian music into his favourite repertoire.)

As well as the modern routine of requiring the services of an efficient impresario, Segovia and Rubinstein also enjoyed "that height of prestige for a musician — and an infallible step towards launching an artistic career" (as Segovia remarked), a measure of royal patronage. In particular the Queen of Spain, grand-daughter of Queen Victoria of England, called Victoria Eugenia, married to Alfonso XIII of Spain, attended all Rubinstein's recitals in Madrid and "would often invite me to play in her royal apartments".

Segovia's account of his own reception at the Royal Palace provides one of his finest anecdotes:

> Following the queen's smiling indication, I took my guitar and played a short programme of pieces which I thought would please my royal listener and her small retinue. At the end, she came towards me, smiling warmly. "Young man, you play like . . . like . . .". She was searching for the words which could best express her pleasure. I waited and at last she found them:
>
> ". . . Like a music box!"
>
> I bowed, smiling to myself, but nevertheless aware of her delicate compliment.
>
> "I have yet to reach that point of perfection, Your Majesty," I said.
> "How modest!" she exclaimed.
>
> (*Andrés Segovia: an autobiography of the years 1893–1920*, pp. 137–8)

Victoria Eugenia had married Alfonso in 1906, a king who was the target of several assassination attempts throughout his life,the first being on his wedding day. A book published in 1914 by an American writer gives a contemporary view of the queen:

> We thought how the youthful Alfonso, then but twenty, had said to Victoria Eugenia, as the blood of his subjects and hers splashed the white satin of her gown and she thought to faint, "the Queen of Spain never faints". He became the king and his queen dared not falter before

Alfonso XIII, King of Spain and his Queen, Victoria Eugenia, wearing the Spanish Mantilla.

the terrible and beautiful responsibilities of the kingdom. . . .

Queen Victoria is popular or not, according with whom you are talking. . . . Victoria is fair and foreign and has been here but a few years, and cannot forget or give up English customs. Still, she is much admired in court circles, and she deserves admiration among the people, for she lives simply and domestically. And if she does not love bull feasts, at least her example is persuading other ladies of the court away from the *corrida*.

(Keith Clark, *The Spell of Spain,* Boston, USA, 1914.)

In their subsequent careers both pianist and guitarist would perform to other monarchs, princes, presidents and ministers. But with this early combination of wise guidance from Quesada and courtly smiles from royalty, both young men were well placed to go forward to their unique artistic destinies.

Later Segovia was signed up by Ibbs & Tillett, a leading British concert agency for British and Commonwealth concerts (from 1924), and by Sol Hurok for North America from 1943. (Hurok also represented Rubinstein from 1937 onwards.) Though at the time of his first Spanish tour for Quesada the repertoire with which we associate Segovia had not yet been written for him, the first striking victories in the battle for the guitar's establishment as a respectable concert instrument had been gloriously won.

# 7

# SEGOVIA AND GUITAR TECHNIQUE

STUDENTS of music, whether aspirants to the profession or keen amateurs, often gather round great players in the green room after concerts, or on less formal occasions, hoping for some word of advice that will illuminate the secrets of instrumental mastery. The key to the inaccessible citadel of the virtuoso cannot, of course, be acquired quite so easily. But throughout his life Segovia has scattered many useful clues about his practising routines and methods.

He practises five hours a day, each session of work being divided into one and a quarter hours, no longer, and four such sessions a day being sufficient. The individual sessions are themselves interspersed with relaxation and activities such as walking, reading, talking with friends, or quiet reflection. Segovia does not believe that endless hours of practice are particularly useful unless, perhaps, a guitarist is swept away by enthusiasm for a new work just received. But normally well measured periods of work are to be preferred, leaving both physical and mental faculties stretched but not exhausted.

Segovia's own recipe for a musician's success is contained in a letter to Bernard Gavoty, written from New York on 20 December, 1954:

> Few people suspect what the study of an instrument demands. The public watch the music-miracle in comfort, never dreaming of the ascesis and sacrifices which the musician must perform in order to make himself capable of accomplishing it. . . .
>
> Don't you agree with me that there is in the world of Art today a great crisis which threatens the love of work, and that we musicians might set an example of morality in this field? It is impossible to feign mastery of an instrument, however skilful the imposter may be; and it is impossible to achieve mastery unless he who undertakes that adventure supplements the generous gift of the gods by the stern discipline of lifelong practice. . . .

81

But as for us pianists, violinists, 'cellists and guitarists — how many hours of pain and self-abnegation, how many weeks, months and years do we spend polishing a single passage, burnishing it and bringing out its sparkle? And when we consider it "done to a turn", we spend the rest of our life persevering so that our fingers shall not forget the lesson or get entangled again in a brambly thicket of arpeggios, scales, trills, chords, accents and grace notes! And if we climb from that region of technique to the more spiritual sphere of interpretation, what anguish we experience in trying to find the soul of a composition behind the inert notation, and how many scruples and repentings we have before we dare to discover what does *not* lie hidden in the paper!

Apart from this basic credo of the artist's life, Segovia had also indicated in several places the actual mechanism of his approach in more detailed terms than almost any other of the great guitarists. With a few significant exceptions guitar tutors and books of technical exercises written in the twentieth century tend to be written by those whose own prowess on the instrument is open to question; such a situation makes any straightforward advice from Segovia particularly valuable.

On his autobiographical recording *The Guitar and I* (Decca, 1971), Segovia explains how in his early years he found out how to improve his technique by making studies out of parts of newly discovered compositions:

A guitar amateur and a jealous guardian of a number of manuscripts of Tárrega opened his treasure to me. Thanks to him I increased my repertoire and also the new works I found inspired me to intensify my study of technique. Out of difficult passages I made a new exercise. Often I ceased to regard the motif I had chosen as part of a specific work and elevated it to a superior level of studies in which was latent the promise of victory over more general difficulties.

Along with this method of improving technique, Segovia's autobiography reveals that he had worked out the fingerings of diatonic scales for guitar some time before his 1909 debut. His book of *Diatonic Major and Minor Scales* (Columbia Music Co., Washington D.C.) was not published until 1953 though it shaped modern approaches to scale study on the guitar.

In this volume he suggests the "patient study of scales" for two hours a day, considering that one hour of scale practice may be preferable to "many hours of arduous exercises which are frequently futile. The practice of scales enables one to solve a greater number of technical problems in a shorter time than the study of any other exercise". By such practice faulty hand positions can be corrected, whilst "independence and elasticity" of the fingers will be developed through which may come "physical beauty of sound". Segovia warns the aspiring guitarist however that "sonority and its infinite shadings are not the result of stubborn willpower but spring from the innate excellence of the spirit".

*The Guitar and I* recordings, Volumes I and II, refer the listener to various studies by Sor, Aguado, Coste, Giuliani and Tárrega (a complete list is given in the Discography) as well as giving a miniature lesson concerned with technical formulas. The lesson not only emphasises the way to practise scales, involving both slow and fast playing, but gives examples of *Slur Exercises and Chromatic Octaves* (Columbia Music, Washington D.C., 1970) in action. Segovia plays slur exercises on particular formulas involving the use of combinations of fingers of the left hand, as well as the "much more difficult" exercise of slurred scales, leading to "greater strength and fluency in his fingers".

Chromatic octaves, slowly at first then rapidly, are considered "excellent for achieving independence of the fingers of the left hand", whilst "scales are the basic exercises for developing speed and flexibility in both hands and also for increasing the volume of sound."

Segovia prescribes as an essential exercise all the right hand patterns put forward by Mauro Giuliani, presumably in the 120 alternatives offered in the composer's Opus 1 (Schott). With this suggestion he concludes the battery of fundamental technical devices, scales, slurs, chromatic octaves, rudimentary studies and right hand exercises, which have formed the basis of his approach to the disciplining and strengthening of the fingers.

Segovia's edition of *Studies for the Guitar by Fernando Sor* (Edward B. Marks, 1945) is an indication of more advanced techniques he has found the most valuable both musically and technically. The studies have been chosen to achieve "the right balance between the pedagogical purpose and the natural musical beauty". His preface to the selected studies is virtually a check list for competence, an acknowledgement of those skills which the guitarist, like any other instrumentalist, most urgently needs to master:

The studies of Sor which are published here can be used not only for the development of the technique of the student, but as well for the preservation of it at its heights for the masters. They contain the exercises of the arpeggios, chords, repeated notes, legatos, thirds, sixths, melodies in the higher register and in the bass, interwoven polyphonic structures, stretching exercises for the fingers of the left hand, for the prolonged holding of the *cejilla* and many other formulas, which, if practised with assiduity and intelligence, will develop vigour and flexibility in both hands and will finally lead to the better command of the instrument.

Also in this preface Segovia cites the work of Scarlatti and Chopin as being representative of composers who unite technical development with musical quality. Segovia clearly dislikes spending time on inferior musical material and wishes the student to be enthusiastic about the composers on whom much time is lavished. His preface to the *Douze Études* of Heitor Villa-Lobos (Max Eschig, Paris, 1953, composed 1929) voices the same preoccupations. Once again he remarks how Scarlatti and Chopin achieve "didactic ends without a suspicion of aridity or monotony" and through such studies fingers can achieve the three aims of "flexibility, strength and independence". Villa-Lobos has thus combined "formulas of astonishing effectiveness for developing technique of both hands" with "disinterested musical beauty".

As Joaquín Rodrigo comments in his tribute, Segovia has devoted many hours of his life to teaching. Contrary to popular belief, perhaps due to Segovia's own often repeated statement that "I am my own master and my own pupil", his teaching activities have been underestimated. He has given many Master Classes and a multitude of private lessons, the latter being offered without payment but with a fervent dedication to the cause of the guitar.

An individual lesson with Segovia is conducted very much in the Spanish style, the emphasis being on the sounds produced, the interpretation required, rather than on basic details of technique. However the procedure is complicated and, as in all tuition, technique and interpretation will merge indissolubly at certain points during the teaching. But Segovia's main concern is to shape and mould the interpretation of specific pieces leaving the student with the responsibility of producing the required sonorities.

Segovia is adept at explaining interpretative points verbally, by singing the exact phrasing of the melodic line, naming the notes as he sings. His own concept of each phrase, conjunction of notes, slurs or effects is total and the subtlety of his ear allows no deviation. His tenacity in pursuing the desired result is that of the conscientious teacher who wishes to see the student achieve the objective. Frequently he compliments and encourages where the playing is to his liking, but swoops like a hawk when the musical line is inappropriately voiced.

Sometimes the student is allowed to play a piece in its entirety but in the next may not be permitted to play past the first few bars. Occasionally Segovia will play the passage under discussion and once the musical intent has been clearly established, advises the student to practise each bar thirty or forty times; he is aware that such practise will be futile if the student has not already grasped the precise idea of the effect required.

Surprisingly, perhaps, Segovia has never himself systematized his technique in terms of a Guitar Method. His views on these matters are either implicitly contained in prefaces and his many editions with detailed fingering, or explicitly conveyed to students who have played for him, or transmuted through the expression of others such as Vladimir Bobri in *Segovia Technique*. This publication deals with the sitting position, the placing of right and left hands, apoyando and tirando techniques, use of nails, right hand technique, left hand placing, barré techniques and pizzicato, with large photographs of Segovia's hands and an explanatory text.

The aim of Bobri's book is "to preserve an indisputable record of this technique, as developed and practised by Andrés Segovia, and to serve as a visual and textual guide in establishing a solid *foundation* for playing technique by aspiring students". Thus the actual value of the book is mainly to offer evidence of the maestro's hand positions and posture, and to correct obvious faults in the fundamental stages rather than to develop technique.

A thorough analysis of Segovia's interpretative methods accompanied by an explanation of relevant techniques is contained in *The Art of Classical Guitar Playing* by Charles Duncan and in an extended article by the same author entitled "The Segovia Sound, What is it?" published in *Guitar Review* No. 42, the autumn edition of 1977.

In his comments Charles Duncan explores the concept of Segovia's tone and discovers that it may not after all be an "impenetrable mystery" but is the product of a "coherent technique". The right hand technique first touches the string and then plays in what the author calls "the principle of the prepared attack". For this the nails of the right hand must obviously be correctly shaped and filed. But the Segovian sound is seen not just as a beautiful sonority but as "a style of interpretation characterized by maximum expressive variety through a well-nigh total control of tonal resources".

These resources involve a specific use of the musical ingredients of dynamics, timbre and rhythm, as well as the exclusion of unnecessary or extraneous non-musical sound. Charles Duncan's exploration is perhaps the most perceptive analysis in print of Segovia's essential style:

> In general, Segovia's style is characterized by a systematic use of staccato. It can be heard in his handling of short single notes; or in motivic fragments composed of short notes. . . . Aesthetically the overall effect is that of extremely distinct musical pronunciation. . . . Segovia's playing is also characterized by a very flexible concept of pulse, which more than any other single factor accounts for the sheer vitality of his sound.
>
> (*Guitar Review,* No. 42, 1977)

The persuasive subtlety of Charles Duncan's probing is very detailed and cannot be best conveyed by selective quotation. In particular his linking of the techniques of Segovia's right hand movements with the fundamental interpretative vision is most expertly achieved. It is rare in guitar writing that such investigation is attempted on the stylistic characteristics of individual players and even rarer that it should be carried off so sympathetically and informatively.

Perhaps the last word on Segovia's technique should be left with one of the world's great players of a later generation who is uniquely qualified to recognize the distinction of the Maestro. Speaking on a BBC programme entitled *Segovia — Celebration* in August, 1974, Julian Bream commenting on a recital by Segovia he attended at the Prince of Wales Theatre, London, shortly after the war, had this to say:

> I was simply riveted by his playing. I'd never heard such beautiful articulation, such a wealth of tone-colour and such wonderfully integral interpretation. His technique is really quite formidable. There's

never been a technique of such precision and control before Segovia and it would be remarkable if there would be in the future a superior technique. He has of course wonderful natural attributes, he has large hands, rather podgy in fact, with fine tapering finger-tips. He has immense power in these hands — this is of great importance because you need tremendous strength to hold down the left hand, particularly in chordal passages. He also has an incredible right hand, in as much that it has great power, is extremely supple and very relaxed. I think the most remarkable thing on hearing Segovia would be the effect of the sound that he produces and the effect of that sound upon one's sensibilities. It is very clear, it is extremely fine, and if one may use the word, aristocratic. Whatever Segovia does, even if occasionally one raises an eyebrow, by way of his phrasing or his taste, nevertheless it's done with terrific conviction and I think it is the hallmark of Segovia's playing that anything Segovia attempted was always done with tremendous conviction.

A drawing by Lorenzo López Sancho showing those personalities who were present in Granada at the *Concurso de Cante Jondo*, 14 June 1922. (Courtesy of Manuel Orozco Díaz.)

1. Diego Bermúdez ('El Tenazas') 2. Ramón Montoya, 3. Joaquín Cuadrados, 4. Pastora Pavón ('Niña de los Peines'), 5. Valentín Felip Durán, 6. El Niño del Barbero, 7. La Niña de la Aguadera, 8. Andrés Segovia, 9. José Ruiz Almadóvor, 10. José Sánchez Puertas, 11. Ruperto Martínez Rioboó, 12. Antonio López Sancho, 13. Ignacio Zuloaga, 14. José García Carrillo, 15. Fernando Vilchez, 16. Manuel de Falla, 17. Vicente León Callejas, 18. Federico García Lorca, 19. Hermenegildo Lanz, 20. José Martínez Rioboó, 22. Ramón Martínez Rioboó, 23. Martínez Rioboó, 23. Santiago Rusiñol, 24. Antonio Ortega Molina, 25. José Carazo, 26. Rogelio Robles Pozos, 27. Francisco Vergara Cardona, 28. Fernando de los Ríos, 29. Santos Martínez, 30. Miguel Cerón, 31. Ramón Carazo.

# 8

# SEGOVIA AND FLAMENCO

SEGOVIA'S relationship with the art of flamenco has had little attention from critics who have generally assumed, from chance remarks of his, that he is not altogether sympathetic to Andalusia's characteristic music. Just as in classical music there is a division between the vocabulary of the avant-garde and the tonalities used by more traditional composers, so there has been a corresponding schism in the ranks of flamenco. Segovia has remained loyal in both classical and flamenco to the older values and in his early career was well acquainted with maestros of flamenco such as Ramón Montoya, Pastora Pavón (La Niña de los Peines), Manolo de Huelva, Manolo Caracol and many other fine artists.

Given Segovia's childhood environment, with its daily exposure to the colours of *cante* and instrumental flamenco, it seems unlikely that Segovia could have disliked it in its native habitat. It is more likely that he was in his youth quite partial to the fine manifestations of *el arte,* as flamenco is often called. But his distaste for more recent developments, often shared by older flamenco players, has been strongly expressed on numerous occasions.

Segovia actually took part in 1922 in *El Concurso de Cante Jondo* (Competition for *cante jondo* or flamenco singing) organized in Granada by Manuel de Falla, and his role was not simply that of a participant in the Festival's fringe activities, which included poetry reading by Federico García Lorca, and an exhibition of the paintings of Ignacio Zuloaga, as well as classical guitar recitals. D.E. Pohren in *Lives and Legends of Flamenco,* remarks that Segovia "who played flamenco as well as classical at that time", was one of the judges of the competition. Félix Grande in *Memoria del Flamenco* refers to Segovia's playing of a *solea,* a flamenco dance; Segovia has published a transcription of some variations on *soleares* "collected during his distant youth" in *Guitar Review* No. 42.

Manuel de Falla feared that the traditional forms of flamenco song were under threat and likely to disappear altogether. The rules of the contest stipulated that the songs were to consist of items such as the *siguirillas gitanas, serranas, polos, cañas* and *soleares,* long established structures of the folkloric culture, whilst a special category was organized for songs to be sung without guitar accompaniment. Singers of both sexes could take part, but professionals over the age of twenty-one were prohibited.

Directions to competitors stressed the importance of the classical values of *cante jondo*:

> We have to warn competitors most earnestly that preference will be given to those whose styles abide by the old practice of the classical *cantaores* and which avoids every kind of improper flourish, thus restoring the *cante jondo* to its admirable sobriety, which was one of its beauties, and is now regrettably, lost.
>
> For the same reasons, competitors should bear in mind that modernized songs will be rejected, however excellent the vocal qualities of the performer. Likewise, competitors should remember that it is an essential quality of the pure Andalusian *cante* to avoid every suggestion of a concert or theatrical style. The competitor is not a singer, but a *cantaor.*
>
> *(Manuel de Falla: On Music and Musicians,* pp. 115–16.)

The purity and directness of Manuel de Falla's vision of folk art was followed up by further stern comments:

> That rare treasure, the pure Andalusian song, not only threatens to disintegrate, but is on the verge of disappearing permanently. Something even worse is happening: with the exception of some *cantaor* still singing, and a few *ex cantaores* with no voice left, what we can usually hear of the Andalusian song is a sad, lamentable shadow of what it was, of what it should be. The dignified hieratic song of yesterday has degenerated into the ridiculous *flamenquism* of today.
>
> *(Manuel de Falla: On Music and Musicians,* p. 116.)

These warnings about a dying art could perhaps equally have applied to the art of flamenco guitar playing. Falla was concerned that *cante jondo* was in transition from an inward, sensitive, unsophisticated artistry, to a state of crowd-pleasing exhibitionism. A trip to the modern flamenco shows for tourists is a sign that Falla's fears for Andalusian art were fully justified. In the context of commercial flamenco, spectacle is paramount, content minimal.

Other sources shed interesting light on the *Concurso;* Falla's biographer, Jaime Pahissa, devotes a useful paragraph to the event:

Antonio Chacon, one of the great flamenco singers.

Pastora Pavón ('Niña de los Peines'), one of the great flamenco artists who was present at the *Concurso de Cante Jondo*.

Ramon Montoya, acknowledged by Segovia as one of the truly great flamenco guitarists.

While Falla was working to complete *The Puppet Show,* the *cante jondo* competition was held in Granada (June 13th and 14th, 1922). Among the judges were Federico García Lorca and Manuel Ángeles Ortiz, who like so many others is now in South America, where he has been living in Buenos Aires since 1939. These two hunted in outlying districts and small villages for the few who could remember the original authentic *cante jondo* songs, rather than the professional singers from cafés and concert halls. The competition was held in one of the great squares, which had been decorated by Ángeles Ortiz, before a huge crowd in which the ladies wore the costume of the early nineteenth century. Falla wrote an introduction for this competition in which he explained the reasons for holding it.

*(Manuel de Falla, His Life and Works.)*

Eduardo Molina Fajardo's book *Manuel de Falla y el Cante Jondo* gives a full account of how one of the singers, Diego Bermúdez, (c.1854–1929), nicknamed "El Tenazas" (The Pliers), had walked for three days from Puente Genil to get to Granada in time for the *Concurso.* "El Tenazas" was well over sixty years of age.

After a performance by a great flamenco *cantaor,* Antonio Chacon, at a café in Granada a day before the contest, with Manuel de Falla, Pastora Pavón, Ignacio Zuloaga and other distinguished artistic personalities present, Bermúdez began to sing. Though one of his lungs had been put out of action during a knife fight many years before, the profundity and inspiration of his singing won the hearts of all. In true fairy-tale style, "El Tenazas" was awarded a prize at the *Concurso* the next day, sharing the honours with an eleven year old gypsy boy later destined for high esteem, Manolo Caracol. Three great guitarists accompanied the singers — Manolo de Huelva, Ramón Montoya and José Cuéllar.

There is a fascinating postscript to this story revealed by Andrés Segovia in *Guitar Review* No. 42, 1977. In a letter to Vladimir Bobri, dated 5 February 1977, Segovia gives a long account of the *Concurso.* In particular it turned out that Diego Bermúdez had been a servant in the household of Segovia's uncle and had been with the family for twelve or fifteen years. On reflection, therefore, it would appear that Segovia's knowledge of *cante jondo* was not arbitrary but was the result of listening during his youth to one of the finest traditional *cantaores* of history, which casts a rather different complexion on the nature of Segovia's relationship with Andalusian folk music.

93

In an interview in the same issue of *Guitar Review* with Vladimir Bobri, Segovia explains how his flamenco favourites include La Niña de los Peines and Manolo de Huelva, one of the legendary guitarists of flamenco:

> Manolo de Huelva played in a *very* simple manner, very flamenco, just as it should be, being folklore. He never resorted to a cheap display of pyrotechnics; his playing was simple, emotional and expressive. . . . Yes, Manolo de Huelva was the best during the time of my youth.

In similar terms to Manuel de Falla's flamenco manifesto, Segovia takes the opportunity to define his ideal of true flamenco:

> I love the flamenco, but the *true* flamenco — not the flamenco heard these days. The flamenco guitarist of today has removed his attention from the ideals of yesterday when this noble art was prized for a depth of emotion which could be produced by a certain simplicity of approach. Today's guitarists are more theatrical, they want to show their technique, to dazzle the public with pyrotechnics. And so they not only insert chords not belonging to the true flamenco, but they also emphasise the rapid scale passages, tremolos, and so forth. The result is not to my taste.

Segovia's views on the matter were also set out in an article in *Music and Musicians* in 1973 in which he names various flamenco guitarists of today whose development he does not admire:

> When asked for a *pronunciamento* on the new wave of flamenco guitarists — Serranito, Manolo Sanlúcar, Paco de Lucia — who currently dominate the *tablao* scene, Segovia replied: "We have never before had such a magnificent assortment of flamenco guitarists. They are marvellous every one of them. The problem is that none of them plays flamenco. How can you expect them to play flamenco? Who understands flamenco? This art is felt and understood by a tiny group of Andalusians — not even by the average Spaniard, mind you — and foreign audiences certainly have no idea of what flamenco means."

Ironically it is possible that Segovia's own liberation of the guitar from the intimate salon atmosphere to the great concert halls of the world may have contributed to a desire by flamenco players to achieve the same kind of success. At one time flamenco could be heard at its best in private *juergas,* gatherings where enthusiasts

94

could celebrate the finer points of *el arte*. But eventually flamenco guitarists began to give recitals in concert halls like their classical counterparts, though sometimes instead of just playing solo guitar they took with them singers and dancers.

One such player, born about 1905, was Carlos Montoya, nephew of the great Ramón Montoya. Of his public image D.E. Pohren remarks:

> What contradictory reactions that name evokes. For thousands of record and concert fans he is Mr Flamenco Guitar. When brought up in professional conversation, however, he is nearly always dismissed with a shrug.
>
> This contradiction again points out that in flamenco, as in all arts, one's tastes must be cultivated. This is further complicated by the fact that even within the professional flamenco world there are widely varying opinions due to the existence of the two schools, the traditional and the modern.

Just as several things had to change when the classical guitar moved from salon to concert hall, so even more startling consequences assaulted the art of flamenco. Transplanted out of its native realm into a variety of alien settings, which included nightclubs, television shows, and tourist spots, as well as the formal concert setting, the emphasis necessarily became focussed on brilliance, on fast-moving exciting rhythms, affecting *cantaor,* dancer and guitarist alike. Once the poison of exhibitionism had crept in, even if the whole world had now become aware of flamenco, it was difficult to see how the art could ever purge itself of such impurity.

The dance also suffered, becoming erotic, revealing, and quite different from the austere expression of inner emotion. Segovia expressed his view of the change in this way:

> What relationship, for example, with the true popular art of Andalusia, with its subtly concealed passion, has the flamenco dancer of today? Her dance consists of flinging her mop of hair over her face, clicking her heels round the stage like a cowboy, and rotating her waist in suggestive movements which evoke the eroticism of tropical countries. Flamenco dance has been always passionate, never obscene, always sensual, never sexual; with grace and elegance. It excited desire, but never by wanton looks and gesture incited its immediate realization.
>
> (*Guitar Review,* No. 42, 1977.)

95

For Manuel de Falla and those who took part in the *Concurso,* the event was in a sense a failure. Instead of becoming an annual occurrence where the purity of the art could be reasserted, flamenco had to wait several decades before similar festivals were organized in Andalusia. In the onward rush of commercialism there are still young players who are mindful of the potential loss of the expressive capability of *el arte* and who wish to keep flamenco true to its great traditions. Many of them do not find themselves in fundamental disagreement with the views of Manuel de Falla and Andrés Segovia, though to retrace footsteps to a golden age remembered is not altogether possible.

Meanwhile that competition, in Granada, with the ladies dressed in nineteenth century costume, through which so many artists (including a great composer, a great poet, and a great classical guitarist, as well as the finest flamenco players), attempted to keep alive the magnificent folkloric culture of Andalusia, can be remembered as one of the finest manifestations of the Spanish sensibility.

# 9

# THE CULTURAL BACKGROUND TO THE AUTOBIOGRAPHY

SEGOVIA'S autobiography reveals his close association with many writers, poets, dramatists and painters during his early years in Granada, Córdoba, Seville and Madrid. To the English-speaking reader most of these figures are obscure or unknown even though some of the writers mentioned are a significant part of Spanish literary life in the early twentieth century.

With the exception of a few Hispanophiles such as Ernest Hemingway, Roy Campbell, Robert Graves and Laurie Lee, European and North American writers have largely remained untouched by Spanish and South American literature. Next to the universal appeal of Miguel de Cervantes Saavedra whose Don Quixote remains one of the best known of all imaginative characters, the poetry of Federico García Lorca has been best loved and most read by the world outside Spain. But over recent years South American writers such as Pablo Neruda, Jorge Luis Borges and Gabriel García Márquez have become increasingly popular in northern Europe and the United States. Yet Spanish literature of the highest quality still tends to be neglected with the result that there is an almost total lack of awareness outside the Latin world of its intensity and richness.

A casual reader of Segovia's autobiography may not, therefore, be in a position to make much sense of the influences, literary and otherwise, which contributed to the guitarist's own development. Spanish is a language not often taught in European schools, especially in Britain, and many Europeans, despite frequent visits to the tourist areas of Spain, remain in the dark about its culture, history and people.

Some British reviewers of Segovia's autobiography expressed their confusion on this matter openly. Meredith Oakes, writing in the *Guardian* remarked:

If Segovia continues his autobiography, as he promises to do, later volumes will have the advantage of containing more familiar names: one gets rather lost in the Spanish mixture of café intellectuals, boyhood friends, guitar heroes, good families and the daughters of good families.

The comment about café intellectuals could surely only come from a reviewer who had not heard the philosopher Miguel de Unamuno's remark that Spanish culture is to be found more in the café than in the university, and café culture has not been negligible in France and Germany either. But in fact the names of Segovia's acquaintances in the Café de Levante, Madrid, where writers and bohemians gathered, are vital to twentieth century Spanish letters.

These include Jacinto Benavente (1866–1954), winner of the Nobel Prize for Literature 1922, Ramón María del Valle-Inclán (1866–1936), Pedro Salinas (1891–1951), and elsewhere in the autobiography, Juan Ramón Jiménez (1881–1958), Nobel Prize winner in 1956, and José Ortega y Gasset (1883–1955).

Andrés Segovia, unlike some dedicated musicians, has always been receptive to literature and art. In his early teens he became attracted to the work of Angel Ganivet (1865–98) whose book *Granada la Bella* he found among the possessions of his uncle Eduardo. Ganivet, not well known at all to English readers was an important influence on the so-called "Generation of '98", a group of leading writers and thinkers who were eager to define the role and identity of contemporary Spain as the twentieth century approached and political events altered Spain's former imperial status.

In 1898 a war between Spain and the United States removed the last vestiges of the once enormous Spanish Empire. In the subsequent Treaty of Paris (10 December 1898), after the Spanish fleet had lost several important battles, Spain gave up sovereign rights over Cuba and Puerto Rico, and ceded the Philippine Islands and other territories to the USA; only small areas of North and West Africa now remained under the Spanish flag. The loss of Empire imposed a humiliation on Spanish pride which was deeply traumatic. The Generation of 1898 hoped to achieve a cultural and ideological renaissance in their country.

The effect of the war with the United States on Spanish thought was analysed in a book published in 1908 by Havelock

98

Ellis, (later famous for his publication *The Psychology of Sex*):

> The war which deprived Spain of the last relics of that empire on which once "the sun never set" has exerted a twofold influence on the Spanish people. On the one hand it has had a definite material effect in enabling Spaniards to devote their energies to the task of working out their economic salvation. On the other hand it has had a less obvious influence of a more spiritual character. It has induced those Spaniards who hold that a nation can only be great by its moral and intellectual distinction, by its fidelity to its own best instincts, to set themselves a task of national self-analysis and self-criticism. What is the real spirit of Spain? these men seem to ask themselves; what is the nature of her great traditions? How can we modern Spaniards learn to become faithful to that spirit and those traditions? To what extent are we wise in doing so?
>
> (*The Soul of Spain*, London, 1908.)

Havelock Ellis then goes on to talk about Angel Ganivet, perhaps the leader of the group "for his book appeared before the war and has not been excelled by any that has appeared since". The book referred to is Ganivet's *Idearium español* (later to be translated by J.R. Carey as *Spain: an Interpretation*, London, 1946) which set out to discover what was wrong with Spain.

Havelock Ellis summed up Ganivet's conclusions about the state of Spain as follows:

> Ganivet's diagnosis of the disease from which his country is suffering — for nearly all intellectual Spaniards seem to agree that there is a disease, though they differ as to its nature and gravity — is *aboulia* or lack of willpower. And though his training was so cosmopolitan, he seeks the remedy in Spain's own native force. "The central motive of my idea," he declares, "is the restoration of the spiritual life of Spain."

Ganivet's life certainly had been cosmopolitan. After obtaining a doctorate in philosophy from Madrid University, he entered the consular service and was posted to duty at Antwerp, Helsinki and Riga. After an unhappy love affair he drowned himself in the River Dvina, near Riga, in 1898 at the age of thirty-three.

As a young man, Segovia went to visit one of Ganivet's close relatives. Here a romantic friendship developed with Encarnación, eight years older than himself. This relationship ultimately ended when Encarnación, under financial pressure from her family, married a "more prosperous admirer" than Segovia.

Though he does not discuss the deeper implications of Ganivet's writings, Segovia could not have been unaware of the relevance of the forceful nationalism being defined by writers and musicians at the turn of the century. In music particularly the work of Felipe Pedrell, Isaac Albéniz and Enrique Granados had achieved a spiritual renaissance which reaffirmed Spanish confidence in its own cultural heritage. This movement was carried forward by the leading lights of the twentieth century such as Manuel de Falla, Joaquín Turina, Federico Moreno Torroba and Joaquín Rodrigo. Spanish composers and instrumentalists returned to their native roots and by creating a specific musical vocabulary forged a clear Spanish voice.

At the end of the nineteenth century and beyond, this process had affected many countries. In Russia the work of Borodin, Mussorgsky and Rimsky-Korsakov (though Tchaikovsky was regarded by his contemporaries as more "westernized"), in Norway the compositions of Grieg, in Czechoslovakia Smetana, and in England the compositions of Elgar, Delius and Vaughan Williams — all these were precise manifestations of nationalist art.

Ganivet's dream of the restoration of the "spiritual life of Spain" would eventually be destroyed in the minds of artists, musicians and writers by the carnage and outcome of the Spanish Civil War. That conflict brought about the deaths of over 750,000 people and the exile of many great Spaniards, including Picasso, Casals, Falla, Jiménez and Machado. Yet, until that dreadful time Spain, unlike the rest of Europe, enjoyed peace, allowing many cultural and spiritual forces space and time to create durable Spanish contributions to art of all kinds.

Of course some Spaniards saw the horrors of the 1914–18 War for themselves. One such was Ramón María del Valle-Inclán, a prolific writer of short stories and novels, who appears in the café society of Madrid at the time Segovia was there. Segovia complains of the man's "insensitivity to musical sound, like that of most Spanish men of letters . . . the musicians, needless to say, understandably felt they were being insulted by this magnificent, garrulous and nonsensical enemy of music".

The Chilean poet Pablo Neruda is equally disapproving of Valle-Inclán:

I saw Valle-Inclán only once. Very thin, with an endless white beard and a complexion like a yellowing page, he seemed to have walked out of one of his own books, which had pressed him flat.

(*Memoirs*, London, 1974)

Valle-Inclán became a war correspondent in 1916 for *El Imparcial*, an experience which altered a former inclination to glorify war. He had been wounded in a café quarrel and this had made necessary the amputation of his left arm. He is best known for his *esperpento* novels in which the characters are viewed as grotesque puppet or doll-like figures. He died in 1936, having rejected Catholicism and professing Communism. Since that time his reputation in Spain has risen, though to non-Spaniards he is virtually unknown.

Particularly prominent at the Café de Levante was Jacinto Benavente, whom Segovia describes as "surrounded by wild admirers" and "the frequent target of enemies and detractors". Jacinto Benavente y Martínez had originally studied law at Madrid University but after his father's death he dedicated himself to writing. By the time Segovia reached Madrid Benavente had written well over fifty plays and between 1908 and 1912 also contributed a weekly column to *El Imparcial*. In 1909 Benavente founded a Children's Theatre for which he wrote several works.

Critics attacked his plays so much that between 1920 and 1924 he even gave up writing drama, though the award of the Nobel Prize in 1922 soothed the wounds, and by the end of his life Benavente had produced 172 plays, completing the last three in 1954, the year of his death.

A clue to the cultural atmosphere in the 1890's can be found in the response to Benavente's most serious play *El nido ajeno* which was booed off the stage in 1894. The critic of *El Imparcial* thought one scene of the play was both obscene and unrealistic; two brothers discuss their mother's possible infidelity to their father. After this debacle Benavente settled for a more congenial type of social satire, a formula which won him popular acclaim and more critical abuse, this time for not reflecting the reality of Spanish life.

Two poets well known to Segovia were Francisco Villaespesa (1877–1935) "many of whose sonnets I knew by heart at that time", and Pedro Salinas, mentioned previously, "whose poetic fire, to me, was more like smouldering embers than a burning

101

flame". Villaespesa, highly influenced by French poetry, was described by Luis Cernuda, a disciple of Salinas and a major poet himself, as "the bridge over which modernism passes to a new generation of writers". Villaespesa evokes melancholy landscapes in twilight or sad autumn rain. He was influential in helping several young poets at the start of their career, the most notable of these being Jiménez. Unfortunately his verse, as Segovia implies, seems not to have stood the test of time and today he is not much read.

Salinas (1891–1951) has been described by the translator and critic J.M. Cohen as "a poet of fine shades and absences, a delicate love-poet". His final poems were depressed contemplations on the nature of the modern world under the shadow of the Bomb. After the Civil War Salinas chose the path of exile and never returned to his homeland.

Another writer destined to be a Nobel Prize winner and well known to Segovia was Juan Ramón Jiménez (1881–1956). At a party in Seville (about 1910) where painters, poets and patrons of the arts had gathered to hear Segovia perform, he met Jiménez "with his sad large expressive eyes and thick beard, his soft curt laugh, so very short that his features would settle back instantly into his unfailing expression of tranquil, poetic melancholy".

Many years later Mario Castelnuovo-Tedesco was to compose twenty-eight pieces for narrator and guitar based on the text of Jiménez's prose poem *Platero y Yo*. From this music Segovia culled ten pieces to make up an attractive suite. This recording made many non-Spaniards aware of Jiménez's writing and several editions of *Platero y Yo,* the story of a donkey and his owner in the Andalusian village of Moguer, have become available in English translation.

Jiménez's gentle melancholy was partly due to bad health which dogged him throughout his life. He was born at Moguer, fifty kilometres or so from Seville, near Huelva on the Gulf of Cádiz, where his house is now a museum and a library of relevant works. He was awarded the Nobel Prize in 1956, an occasion that turned to sorrow when his wife Zenobia died a few days later.

Jiménez, too, was forced into exile by the Civil War, living in various countries including Puerto Rico, Cuba and the United States. His *Platero y Yo* has also been celebrated in the guitar music of Eduardo Sainz de la Maza. The light romanticism of this poetic work evokes the pastoral innocence of the old Spain.

It should be clear from these brief outlines that the personalities who appear in Segovia's autobiography, though they may be largely unknown to many English readers, are certainly not insignificant in Spanish literature and deserve to be more widely read. Segovia's preference for various poets was quoted in the *Sunday Telegraph* in October 1981, in an article by Philip Purser:

> I like philosophy, history, poetry, and best of all the poetry of — can you guess? Not Lorca but Antonio Machado, the greatest poet of our time.

Antonio Machado (1875–1939) remains one of the most admired of all modern Spanish poets. He died in France of pneumonia after fleeing over the Pyrenees with his mother and other refugees of the Civil War. Of him Pablo Neruda remarked:

> I saw Don Antonio Machado several times, sitting in his favourite café dressed in his black notary's suit, silent and withdrawn, as sweet and austere as an old Spanish tree.

*(Memoirs)*

It is a potent image, brooding and intense, which in brief captures the inner dignity of this great Spaniard. The reputation of Antonio Machado continues to grow as his stature as a poet and as a symbol of the true voice of Andalusia is recognized in many critical and biographical works.

The complex web of Andrés Segovia's cultural background is sketched in lightly and unpretentiously in the autobiography. The untroubled ebullience of life in Madrid during the early decades of the century was a fruitful environment for a young man of sensitivity, for the Spanish scene at the time was a ferment of many kinds of artistic activity. The sheer profusion of artists, poets, and musicians, philosophers, dramatists, and critics, denotes what a crucial period this was in the cultural life of Spain.

Following 1939 the hopes of earlier decades were crushed by oppressive censorship. Lorca's murder, Machado's death, the departure of Picasso, Casals, Segovia, Falla, Salinas, Jiménez and many others, was a traumatic watershed in the creative life of Spain. But the Spanish renaissance, yearned for by Ganivet and the Generation of 1898, despite waste and loss, had indeed to a large extent born fruit

# 10

# IMAGES OF SEGOVIA

SEGOVIA'S relationships with the press have been extremely cordial. His ability to win over writers and interviewers and to respond to them as individuals has resulted in many affectionate essays about his life and work. The popular press as well as the more specialist musical periodicals have discovered that Andrés Segovia always provides fascinating material whether in the form of engaging anecdotes or in more probing attempts to capture something of his personality.

To describe the atmosphere at the start of a recital by Segovia is often the opening gambit of a successful article. The prototype of all such descriptions was Bernard Gavoty's account in his book *Segovia*:

> . . . This was the castle of La Brede — near Bordeaux — a château encircled by its moat, with the water sparkling in the June sunshine, and beyond by flowery meadows. A spring breeze was nudging with demure little puffs at the barred windows of the library where Segovia was going to perform before an invited audience of 400. Within these dark old walls the air was pleasant, almost cool despite the time of year. A platform had been erected for the occasion and two seats placed on it, one of ordinary size, the other very low; a chair with a high back, and a little stool of solid wood. . . .
>
> And there he is: he comes forward, carrying his guitar. His prelate-like gravity and natural grandeur accord perfectly with the throne on which he takes his seat. With his left foot on the stool, like a needle-woman, he sets the guitar on his thigh and turns it towards his breast. With his forearm resting on the edge of the sound-board and his right hand between sound-hole and bridge, Segovia contemplates his guitar before beginning to play. . . .
>
> . . . hush! he is beginning!
>
> But has he really begun? That arpeggio sketched by the ball of his thumb has not really stirred the guitar. But he has quietly opened the door to a secret world where everything is caresses, murmurs and silences, a miniature world of which Segovia is the magician.

A writer in *Newsweek*, January, 1959, was attracted by the same magical moment during a recital at New York Town Hall:

The stage is bare except for one square-cushioned piano stool and a small footrest. The spacious hall is brim-full, sold out after one modest advertisement. Suddenly the muted chatter of the expectant audience explodes into rapturous applause as a benign, comfortably padded figure walks out slowly from the wings, settles on the stool, props his foot on the rest and nestles his big shiny guitar against his chest. As he peers out from behind his dark-rimmed glasses and strikes the first delicate chords of an old sixteenth-century air, absolute silence engulfs the audience.

Noel Busch, in a substantial article in *Reader's Digest* of October, 1972, evokes a similar scene:

The concert stage is empty except for an ordinary piano stool and a footstool just under five inches high. About three minutes after the scheduled starting time, a plump, mild-looking septuagenarian dressed in white tie and tails ambles on, carrying a beautiful wooden guitar.

He settles himself comfortably on the piano stool, places his left foot on the smaller stool and looks out at the audience with an expression of benign indulgence. The murmur of conversation subsides, and when total silence has lasted perhaps twenty seconds, his well-muscled fingers begin to move across the strings. From that moment on, listeners experience a unique and unforgettable enchantment. For this is Andrés Segovia, the greatest classical guitarist in the world.

Many have attempted to convey the sense of Segovia's physical presence on or off the concert platform, though it is a difficult thing to describe. The philosopher, Max Nordau, attending a recital by Segovia in 1919 expected to see "a dark haggard man with pronounced features, a vividly coloured belt around his slim hips, a sombrero Cordobes on his head, and a cigarette in the corner of his mouth"; instead he saw a young man "tall, elegant — with long abundant hair leaving a high forehead free. His face beaming with smiling intelligence was strongly suggestive of the 'Bacchus' of Velasquez or of the 'Apollo at the Forge of Vulcan' by the same painter" (*Guitar Review*, No. 4, 1947).

Over fifty years later they were still trying. The *Observer* Review of 10 May 1970, described him as "like an elderly porcelain Cheshire cat; stout and genial with an unnervingly pink skin and a bemused expression". Some years later Sue Arnold of the *Observer* saw him as "a large floppy man, with a soft voice and an old-fashioned courtliness". Alan Kennaugh of the *Radio Times* commented on "the portly gentleman who looks like a benevolent uncle . . . in casual dress with a bootlace bow-tie". An article by Philip Purser in the *Sunday Telegraph* Colour Magazine (October 1981) celebrating the advent of the Segovia International Guitar Competition, offered the readers this:

> The likeness familiar from record sleeves (round face, round spectacles, swept-back hair and Schubertian floppy bow-ties) has been ennobled rather than ravaged by the years. The hair is wispier certainly, the bow more restrained. Under his tweed jacket his trousers reach high above his waist. When he sits down a comfy paunch is apparent. When he laughs, which he soon does, it heaves merrily in agreement.

Segovia's external appearance is so devoid of the eccentric or extraordinary that journalists almost struggle for words to create a sharp, unmistakable impression. His demeanour is distinguished and he could be mistaken for a diplomat, financier or great man of letters; apart from his silver-tipped cane, and in winter the occasional flowing cloak round his shoulders, there is in Segovia's later years little of the ebullient flamboyance of his early appearance. He describes in his autobiography how at the age of eighteen he presented himself at the workshop in Madrid of the guitar maker, Manuel Ramirez, somewhat overdressed for the occasion:

> . . . I was tall and skinny with long black hair flowing under a wide-brimmed hat, tortoise-shell glasses, a wide, full cravat like the one some provincial photographers wear to give themselves artistic airs, a black velvet jacket fastened up to my neck with silver buttons, a long grey double-breasted overcoat, striped pants, patent-leather shoes, and, in my hand, a sturdy cane to further enhance my image.
> (*Andrés Segovia: an autobiography of the years 1893–1920*, pp. 49–50.)

When writers turn from the outward appearance to the inner man, attempts to elucidate the individuality of Segovia are not guaranteed success. With true Andalusian reticence, Segovia's originality does not assert itself in the form of hard-hitting, outspoken views on all and sundry. As Bernard Gavoty remarked after Segovia had trotted out a poetic anecdote about the widow's son of Nain:

> He spoke in such a sincere, natural voice that there could be no suspicion of artificiality. For Segovia does not strive to coin phrases: he

106

expresses his thoughts with the words that come to him, and all else is said with the guitar in his hand.

(Segovia)

Apart from his devotion to the guitar and related topics, Segovia reveals little in interviews about his private feelings or experiences, offering only that which is in the finest sense, impersonal. This reinforces the impression of a fastidious purity, an image of Segovia the man at one with Segovia the musician.

The disciplined moderation of Segovia's personality was forcefully described in the *Daily Express* in 1967:

> "He does nothing to excess," says a friend. "He eats, drinks, reads, looks at and listens to only the best. He does not even practise the guitar to excess, just two and a half hours in the morning, two and a half in the afternoon. The most important word in connection with Segovia is *civilised*."

The same theme is repeated when Philip Purser remarks that Segovia is "the grand old man of civilized Spain" or in the *Observer's* comments of 10 May 1970:

> Segovia is supremely civilized. He drinks only the purest wines, reads only the rarest literature, speaks five languages fluently, but German only in self-defence.

These sentiments are echoed even when the critics discuss the recitals:

> The eternal appeal of Segovia, after listening to him for more than twenty years, is the purity of his music. It is all basic: a performer, an instrument, and the sounds ten fingers can produce on the strings. And the genius of Segovia is that while he is there, we ask for nothing more. The musical line he shapes, its rhythms, harmonies and artistic force, are world enough for our ears.
>
> (Robert C. Marsh, *Chicago Sun-Times*, 20 February 1980.)

> He was able to hold the prolonged attention of a packed Festival Hall despite its being, by all commonsense standards, an absurd place for a guitar recital. That is partly because Mr Segovia's interpretations have a classical purity lacking in the work of younger and more spectacular players.
>
> (Max Harrison, *The Times*, 30 March 1977.)

Segovia's playing, like his off-stage demeanour, is pure and civilized in the sense that all is refinement, and nothing exhibitionist or sensational is ever introduced to attract public attention. His art remains undiluted by self-display or easy appeal to public taste. Such purity is quickly perceived by journalists and admired, though as a follow-up they often elicit Segovia's views on the pop idols of the day, the electric guitar, and amplification of his own guitar. Such questions are like asking a great Shakespearean actor why he does not use a microphone in the theatre or a painter why he does not prefer photography. But Segovia answers these enquiries with courtesy and precision and certainly does not fudge the reply.

That his values as an artist run counter to those of the world of mass entertainment and show business is no secret. Such a discussion can also draw attention to Segovia's concept of the ideal guitar, as reported in the *Daily Express* during the 1960s:

> I would like everyone to listen to the lovely natural voice of the guitar. A guitar should be shaped simply and with a feminine quality, like an honest woman. It should be built to produce many voices, many colours.

Segovia's view of the guitar is rooted in the instrument's natural qualities. He dislikes the way amplification in the concert hall changes timbres from their true sonorities into something false:

> While he plays in large halls and makes himself audible to large audiences, Segovia refuses to use any kind of amplificaton. "It alters the beautiful sound of the guitar, nullifies it, renders it acid and metallic," he says passionately. "From a loudspeaker you can still appreciate the artistry of the performer, the agility of his fingers, but you do not have the true sound of the instrument."
>
> (*International Herald Tribune*, 20 March 1980.)

But Segovia's distrust of pop culture is not founded only on its use of amplification. The movements, the publicity, the audience reaction — all are quite different from what he would regard as the appropriate response to do with art. In the 1960s, when the popularity of the Beatles was at its height, Segovia gave his views on the phenomenon:

> I have heard of these Beatles but what they play is strange to me. I do not think it is anything to do with art as I know it. I do not like the

movements of the boys, the loud electric guitars, the cries, the way the girls go crazy.

I distrust quick popularity. An artist should concentrate on his guitar with all his life and let his public come later. We guitarists — or any serious musicians — need the stern discipline of life-long practice, many years of self-denial.

(*Daily Express.*)

Over fifteen years later writers still show the same interest in Segovia's lack of enthusiasm for electric guitars and their environment. But since the early 1960s pop culture has become a dominant feature in contemporary life; nowadays articles in popular newspapers aimed at a mass audience find it difficult to resist the subtlest implication that it is the solitary figure of the man playing the guitar, natural and unadorned, at the Festival Hall, London, who is a little eccentric, whilst the whirligig of pop with its flashing lights, transient idols and massive amplification is an accepted normality. Moreover it is a bold journalist who can resist some passing deference to the pop world when writing about Segovia:

That pop music has these days made the "little orchestra" the most widely played — or widely strummed — instrument in the western world is something else. Segovia, not unexpectedly, cannot enthuse. He said once that the electric guitar turned a lovely instrument into a monster, and when told of Yehudi Menuhin's desire to unite "beat" and Bach remarked sourly that Menuhin did not have to listen to a world full of electric violins. Nor can he applaud the flirtations with rock groups of his pupil John Williams — "He is doing the reverse of what I did, he is putting the guitar out of classical music again."

(Philip Purser, *Sunday Telegraph,* October 1981.)

Mr Purser does not discuss whether Yehudi Menuhin's good-natured recordings with the great jazz artist Stephane Grapelly are conclusive evidence of a desire to unite "beat" and Bach on a permanent conjugal basis. In fact, Menuhin's views on pop music, though more tolerant perhaps to the Beatles, are very akin to Segovia's. When Yehudi Menuhin attended a pop concert he made the following comments:

I was appalled. The music, if it can be called that, was a kind of torture, calculated to dominate the senses. . . . The sheer volume of sound was overwhelming and it was no consolation to learn afterwards

109

that the amplification system had been faulty. I left before the end because I was feeling so ill at ease.

I don't like to surrender my self-composure: I like to feel that I am in possession of myself and all my faculties. On the other hand, I surrender willingly to Bach, Beethoven or Schubert. . . .

But I couldn't in any way participate in this cheap, noisy, contrived, depersonalizing entertainment, so-called. Thousands of pounds had been spent on the lighting, the sets, the presentation; the group wore clothes covered with sequins and rhinestones which reflected the bright light. From my point of view, the musical content was virtually non-existent. . . .

When I left, the mood of the audience was on the verge of hysteria. Having lived during the time of the Nuremberg rallies, I have a horror of mobs. I was disturbed by this enormous audience of young people, imitating every gesture of the group on stage, their senses and emotions being abused and taunted to produce commercial gain. I feared that, having lost all sense of proportion, the audience could be dominated, coerced. What terrified me was the compulsion towards unanimity.

(*Conversations with Menuhin*, ed. Robin Daniels, London, 1979.)

Menuhin, like Segovia, is particularly interested in the psychology of audience response. A classical recital needs a particular atmosphere within which music reveals itself, emerging from silence and performed to a closely attentive audience. Critics have commented time and time again on the stillness characteristic of audiences at a guitar concert:

Segovia puts the music under a microscope and each little sound, each nuance, shines out in its full beauty and significance against the background of silence of the spellbound audience.

(*Goois Dagblad,* Holland, October 1947.)

He plays for himself. And as he does so you can hear a pin drop, even among three thousand people. . . .

But Segovia's magic is to draw his listeners into a web of silence and for this only the insubstantial and elusive will suffice.

(Stephen Walsh, *The Times,* 30 October 1965.)

. . . Segovia retains his mastery of audience psychology. A quick glance upwards and the packed Festival Hall is silent, coughs suppressed, conscious perhaps of the time when twenty years ago and already a living legend, this great guitarist demonstrated the art of silent coughing to an unfortunate Madrid audience.

(Keith Horner, *The Times,* 21 October 1975.)

That this habit of silence is a long-standing aspect of Segovia's career is proved by Domingo Prat's *Diccionario de Guitarristas* (Romero & Fernandez, Buenos Aires, 1934). Segovia must have learned early on the necessity of accommodating the audience to the gentle sounds of the guitar:

> During the concert he requires a religious silence from the audience; the smallest sound annoys him and he indicates with a subtle gesture that it should not be repeated.

In his autobiography Segovia tells how he checked his first big concert hall, the Palau in Barcelona, for acoustic properties by snapping his fingers from various points in the theatre, and later asked a friend to make certain that guitar sonorities could be heard from any place in the auditorium:

> Contrary to the dire predictions of the opposition, the Palau was nearly full for my recital and the surprised audience found that all they needed to do to hear every work I played was to remain silent and attentive. (p. 121).

Segovia's overall message is at one with his mission. He wished the guitar to be listened to at all times with intelligence and respect. But the affections of the listener need to be retained permanently if the guitar is not to relapse into its former mediocrity. Thus his care for the instrument's welfare is constantly vigilant:

> Segovia cherishes the guitar's traditional values. In an age which has seen and heard them debased beyond belief, he has shown that style and technique need never be compromised to those who seek its true fascination.
>
> (Noel Goodwin, *The Times*, 20 October 1981.)

Segovia has continued throughout his long life to campaign for those traditional values, allowing no dilution of the guitar's identity. To an amazing extent, in a cultural environment far different from that in which Segovia's musical values were formed, this message has penetrated throughout the world and many thousands of players and devotees have followed his lead.

The final word of this chapter may be safely left with a critic of the 1920's, writing after Segovia's debut in Denmark. Through the subsequent decades, writers have returned many times to the same sentiments:

This young Spaniard is really a phenomenon, just as the rumours said. We have never heard anyone who even roughly compares with the way he plays his guitar. With his incredible virtuosity and his tastefulness which proves the high standard of his musical culture, he makes the guitar an instrument on which "proper" music can be performed to a greater degree than one might suppose.

(*Politiken*, Copenhagen, 29 April 1927.)

# 11
# *THE ACHIEVEMENTS*

IT IS NOT EASY to categorize with certainty an instrumentalist's achievements. Unlike a composer who may acquire a reputation with a mere handful of outstanding works, the recitalist depends on a cumulative build-up of concerts and recordings through which to sustain his public esteem over a number of years.

But even here there are obvious pitfalls. An artist's finest recordings may go out of circulation, whilst the greatness of individual records may be less obvious to later generations accustomed to rapid technological progress. The art of interpretation so richly appreciated in one era can become some kind of historical object thirty or forty years on.

In the same way transcriptions, musical translations from one medium to another so beloved by guitarists, eventually need re-thinking. As Segovia remoulded some of the arrangements of Tárrega and others, so today's guitarists are apt to scrutinize the works featured in Segovia's recitals and publish their own versions of pieces he made famous.

Fortunately Andrés Segovia has often expressed in unam-biguous terms the central ambitions of his life. The fruits of his labour have been fulfilled in thousands of recitals, over forty long-playing records, dozen of transcriptions, editions and publi-cations, and the work of many composers who have been inspired to write pieces for him. The usually transient nature of the re-creative artist's daily preoccupations, quite unlike the more durable offerings of composer, writer or artist, has in Segovia's instance become transformed into a permanent part of the con-temporary musical scene. It is therefore worthwhile to look at Segovia's aims to see the distance the guitar has travelled since his first recitals began the long journey to success.

These objectives, expressed with the clarity which distinguish both his music and his speech have been repeated many times in print, broadcasts, and private conversation. They go beyond any suggestion of personal ambition, being instead a desire for the guitar's well-being and a statement of belief from which the guitar

113

can continue to develop and prosper. Such aims transcend the range of ambitions advanced by guitarists before Segovia and provide a necessary combination of incentives for those internationally acclaimed recitalists who, born from 1920 onwards, inherited Segovia's hard-won legacy.

In Segovia's early life neither the course he should steer nor his ultimate destination were apparent:

> From my youthful years I dreamed of raising the guitar from the sad artistic level in which it lay. At first my ideas were vague and imprecise, but as I grew in years and my love for it became intense and vehement, my will to do so became more assertive and my intentions clearer.
>
> (*The Guitar and I*)

> From the beginning of my career I had five purposes aiming to the redemption of the guitar. At first without precision, for I was a boy of nine years old: later, more clearly thought over, when I was getting more familiar with the instrument and its possibilities.
> (from Andrés Segovia's acceptance speech upon receiving the degree of
>     Doctor of Music, Honoris Causa, at Florida State University,
>         Tallahassee, on 27 February 1969.)

The "five purposes", unified in their intent of raising the guitar from mediocrity, are given in *Guitar Review* No. 32, as follows:

1.  To extract the guitar from the noisy and disreputable folkloric amusements. . . . Listening to the persuasive voice of the guitar, I said to myself, "How is it possible that such a beautiful instrument has no serious music composed for it?" My friends came to my rescue by helping me to find the kind of music that I was looking for.

At a time when folk music of many kinds has been acknowledged as a valuable repository of inherited musical wisdom, Segovia's words may at first seem severe. The work of people such as Bartók, Kodály and Grainger in recording folk music either in notation or on early phonographs, and by incorporating such material in their own works, has altered our perspectives for ever. But the invention of radio and the establishment of centralized broadcasting effectively destroyed the isolation, innocence and naivety of the folk singer's art. Paradoxically, the greatness of folkloric material was only appreciated when virtual extinction became a threat.

114

In Segovia's youth the guitar was regarded as being of little serious musical value, fit only for the tavern and considered at the same level of esteem as the penny-whistle or the banjo. The guitar in Spain was everywhere and nowhere. It could be heard in every street, yet despite the efforts of Tárrega and Llobet, was not considered as a serious recital instrument. Segovia's fight was to lift the guitar from the contempt in which it was held. His achievement, often misunderstood, was not to prevent the guitar from being a folkloric instrument but to allow it to assume an extended destiny and a further identity. An aim that was achieved when audiences ceased to find the presence of a guitar in the concert hall ridiculous and composers became willing to think beyond the accepted clichés previously considered appropriate for the guitar.

Aided by his friends, Segovia began the process of research, looking for the music from previous centuries which surely ought to be there. He seemed aware from an early age that like-minded musicians must also have been interested in the guitar's expressive possibilities. His programmes soon incorporated a wide diversity of repertoire, with the available material constantly being refreshed and added to.

Segovia's complex relationships with the folkloric music of Andalusia, flamenco, have already been considered. Yet, it must be emphasised that Segovia's relationship with composers such as Joaquín Turina, Federico Moreno Torroba and Joaquín Rodrigo, as well as his close friendship with Manuel de Falla, enabled Spanish musicians to unite their refinement of folkloric traditions and dances with the voice of the classical guitar.

Thus as Segovia expresses it elsewhere, the guitar became detached from "mindless folk-lore entertainments" yet able to return to what was best and most vital in the culture of Andalusia. Moreover it seems likely that Segovia's success as a concert artist may have inspired flamenco players of high calibre to pursue an international recital career, thus introducing the music of southern Spain to the entire world. Segovia's service to the folkloric music of Andalusia is more profound than usually acknowledged whilst his devotion to the guitar's seriousness ensured that the instrument could not be associated for ever with its previous role of accompaniment or use as a mere background to other activities.

115

2.  I requested the living serious composers not in the field of the guitar to write for me. This was the second of my purposes: to create a wonderful repertoire for my instrument.

A list of the compositions dedicated to Segovia, along with his many transcriptions and editions, appears later in the book. The quality and extent of this body of work constitute the central core of Segovia's achievement. His earnest request in the autobiography, "My kingdom for a repertoire!" has been well attended to.

The initiative which Segovia undertook from the 1920s onwards to seek the help of non-guitarist composers continues to bear fruit still as contemporary musicians hurry to join the ranks of those who have contributed to the instrument's resources. It is now regarded as quite normal for a composer to study the mysteries and challenges of the guitar, usually dedicating the work to one or other of today's leading players.

Of those composers who gave a new repertoire to Segovia, Manuel Ponce was a great favourite. In the New York *Guitar Review* No. 7, 1948, Segovia commented:

> Anyone who loves the instrument — let alone those who have professed its religion — unless he be hard-hearted and empty-headed, must reverence the memory of Ponce. He lifted the guitar from the low artistic state in which it had lain. Along with Turina, Falla, Manén, Castelnuovo-Tedesco, Tansman, Villa-Lobos, Torroba, etc. but with a more abundant yield than all of them put together, he undertook the crusade full of eagerness to liberate the beautiful prisoner. Thanks to him — as to the others I have named — the guitar was saved from the music written exclusively by guitarists.

Even today many guitarists must remain dissatisfied with the available repertoire. The great classical and romantic composers passed by the instrument, a loss no advocacy could redeem in later ages. Yet the "wonderful repertoire" of Segovia's vision exists still in the imagination, and recitalists gratefully accept the legacy of Segovia's years and hope that even more magnificent works may in time be written to fulfil the task Segovia began.

3.  My third purpose was to make the guitar known by the philharmonic public all over the world.

Segovia's international recital career, after his early recitals in

Granada, Seville, Córdoba, Madrid, Barcelona and other Spanish musical centres, began about 1920 with his first tour of various South American countries. In 1924 came the debuts in London and Paris, followed in 1928 by tours of the United States and the Far East, and a trip to Japan in 1929. From that time onwards Segovia's tireless globe-trotting has ensured that most of the world has had a chance to hear his guitar.

4. Another, and fourth purpose, has been to provide a unifying medium for those interested in the development of the guitar. This I did through my support of the now well known international musico-logical journal, the *Guitar Review*, developed by Vladimir Bobri.

From the early nineteenth century onwards, when the periodical *The Giulianiad* was established to commemorate the achieve-ments of the Italian guitarist-composer Mauro Giuliani, classical guitarists have felt the need to discuss and define the instrument and its personalities in its own terms. Until quite recently more broadly based music publications tended to ignore guitar matters altogether, or to deal with them superficially. The *Guitar Review*, founded in New York in 1946, has proved to be one of the enduring scholarly journals in which guitar history could be recorded and analysed. Segovia's autobiography first appeared in serial form in its pages.

The initial aim of the *Guitar Review* was to reclaim "the classical guitar from obscurity and disparagement, so that it may regain its full measure of dignity in the musical world . . . we may before long become proud of our share in the task of rescuing the classical guitar from the undeserved neglect into which it has fallen for more than a century."

Since that time many guitar magazines have flourished through-out the world, several of them inspired by the dedicated and serious tone of *Guitar Review*. Segovia's contribution to the early magazine as a writer and fervent advocate of deeply held beliefs is a vital part of the development of a receptive guitar audience since 1946.

5. I am still working on my fifth and maybe the last purpose, which is to place the guitar in the most important conservatories of the world for teaching the young lovers of it, and thus securing its future.

The walls of musical academe are traditionally well reinforced and radical change does not enter easily. This particular objective was in many instances fulfilled about fifty years or more after Segovia's debut in Granada. When Julian Bream, for example, entered the Royal College of Music, London, in the 1950s there was nobody to teach him the guitar and at one stage he was forbidden to take his instrument into the College building. However, out of such apparent setbacks progress emerges, and since the late 1950s most Colleges of Music throughout the world have begun to offer tuition in guitar.

Segovia defines this objective as a desire "to influence the authorities at conservatories, academies and universities to include the guitar in their instruction programmes on the same basis as the violin, 'cello, piano, etc." It is remarkable that Segovia, who unlike Tárrega did not study music formally at a conservatoire, should acknowledge that the inclusion of the guitar on college syllabuses would bring about a long-term stability in the development of players and teachers of the instrument.

Certainly in recent years the standards of guitar performance, particularly among younger players, have risen amazingly. The Segovia International Guitar Competition, sponsored by the Sherry Producers of Spain, and held at Leeds Castle, Kent, England in October 1981, featured forty-three players under the age of thirty drawn from many countries. Nearly every one of them had attended a conservatory, university or academy of some kind in order to pursue guitar studies in depth. The pedagogic traditions of the guitar which have evolved over the last few decades are now comparable with those of other instruments and will surely continue to progress dynamically and creatively.

# 12

# THE HONOURS

ANDRÉS SEGOVIA has been awarded the following honours in recognition of his services to music:

Created Marquis of Salobreña by His Majesty King Juan Carlos I in 1981

## GRAND CROSSES AND MEDALS
Grand Cross of Isabel la Católica
Grand Cross of Alfonso X el Sabio
Grand Cross of Beneficencia
Cavalier Grand Cross of the Order of Merit of the Italian Republic
Gold Medal for Merit in Achievement
Gold Medal of Fine Arts
Gold Medal of Madrid
Gold Medal of the City of Linares
Gold Medal of the Province of Jaén
Gold Medal of the Province of Granada
Gold Medal of the City of Florence, Italy
G.F. Handel Medal of the City of New York
Gold Medal of the Spanish Institute, New York
Gold Lion of the City of Venice

Honorary Citizen of Linares
Honorary Citizen of Granada
Honorary Citizen of Jaén

## DOCTOR HONORIS CAUSA
Doctor 'Honoris Causa' at the following universities:
University of Oxford, England
University of Santiago de Compostela
Universidad Autónoma of Madrid
University of Granada
University of New Orleans, USA
University of Florida

School of Arts, University of North Carolina
International College of Los Angeles

## APPOINTMENTS
Academician at the following:
The Royal Music Academy of Stockholm
The Academy of Saint Cecilia, Rome
The Academia Filarmonica of Bologna
The Royal Academy of Fine Arts of San Fernando, Madrid
The Fine Arts of Santa Isabel de Hungria, Seville
The Royal Academy of Fine Arts of Nuestra Señora de las
  Angustias, Granada

## PRIZES
The National Music Prize, Spain
"A Life for Music" Prize, Venice
The Leonnie Sonning Prize, Copenhagen
The Ambassadors Prize, San Remo, Italy
The Albert Schweitzer Prize

## MASTER CLASSES
Andrés Segovia has given Master Classes at the following places:
University of Southern California, Los Angeles, California, USA
University of California, Berkeley, USA
North Carolina School of Fine Arts, USA
Academia Musicale Chigiana, Siena, Italy
Santiago de Compostela Summer School "Music at Compostela",
  Spain
The Geneva Conservatory
The Manuel de Falla Foundation, Granada
The Metropolitan Museum of Arts, New York

120

# 13
# DISCOGRAPHY

This discography is in two parts: the first part gives the principal albums recorded by Andrés Segovia and the second, in chronological order of birth, lists individual composers and their works.

Record companies will presumably continue to select and permutate collections of individual pieces to be issued in new albums under different titles. An attempt has been made in this discography to present each album in the format in which it originally appeared. (The exception to this is the collection of 78 rpm's now offered to the public as long-playing records.)

It is not possible, with so many issues being sold, to give a complete list of each record number for every track in all its editions. The following catalogue is a general guide to the recordings of Andrés Segovia, showing the range of composers and the quantity of his work in studios round the world since the 1920s.

Segovia's first recordings were made during 1924–25, at the time of his second concert tour of South America. He first heard his own playing in a studio in Havana. It is not known whether any copy still exists of these early attempts. Many fine copies of 78 rpm recordings commercially issued after 1927 are in the hands of collectors.

**The Art of Andrés Segovia**
The HMV Recordings 1927–39
The HMV Treasury RLS.745 2 LP set

**Side 1**
Gavotte (from Partita No.3 for Violin BWV 1006) J.S. Bach
Courante (from Suite No.3 for 'Cello BWV 1009) J.S. Bach
Prelude (from Suite No.1 for 'Cello BWV 1007) J.S. Bach
Prelude in C minor (No.3 from the Clavier-büchlein for Wilhelm Friedemann Bach BWV 999) J.S. Bach
Allemande (from Lute Suite in E minor BWV 996) J.S. Bach
Fugue in G minor J.S. Bach
Suite in A Ponce/Weiss
    Prelude—Gigue—Sarabande—Gavotte

**Side 2**
Thème varié Op.9 Sor

Sarabande — Bourrée — Menuet de Visée
Gigue Froberger
Allegretto (from Sonatina in A) Torroba
Canzonetta Mendelssohn (arr. Segovia)
Serenata Malats
Recuerdos de la Alhambra Tárrega
Study in A Tárrega
Vivo ed energico (from Sonata Homage to Boccherini) Castelnuovo-Tedesco

**Side 3**
Granada Albéniz
Sevilla Albéniz
Fandanguillo Torroba
Preludio Torroba
Nocturno Torroba
Fandanguillo Turina
Danza Española No.10 in G Op.37 Granados
Danza Española No.5 in E minor Op.37 Granados

**Side 4**
First movement of Sonata III Ponce

121

*Canción* (from Sonata III) Ponce
*Postlude* Ponce
*Mazurka* Ponce
*Petite Valse* Ponce (arr. Segovia)
*Variations and Fugue on 'Folies d'Espagne'*
  Ponce

## Andrés Segovia
The HMV Treasury HLM 7134

**Side 1**
*Guitar Concerto No.1 in D* Op.99
  M. Castelnuovo-Tedesco
  1st movement: Allegro giusto
  2nd movement: Andantino — Alla
  Romanza
  3rd movement: Ritmico e cavalleresco
with the New London Orchestra conducted
by Alec Sherman
(from Col. CAX 10582–87, LX. 1404–6
recorded 11/12 July 1949)

**Side 2**
*Sonatina Meridional* M. Ponce
  1st movement: Campo (Country)
  2nd movement: Copla (Song)
  3rd movement: Fiesta (Feast)
(from Col. CAX. 10574–5, LX. 1275)
*Norteña* J.G. Crespo
(from Col. CA 21152, LB.130)
*Fandanguillo* J. Turina
(from Col CAX. 10569, LX. 1248)
*Arada and Fandanguillo from 'Suite
  Castellana'* F. Moreno Torroba
(from Col. CAX 10568, LX, 1248)
*Two Studies* H. Villa-Lobos
(from Col. CAX. 10567, LX. 1248)
(side 2 recorded between 22 & 30 June 1949)
1978

## Andrés Segovia plays Bach
Saga 5248

**Side 1**
*Gavotte* from 'Cello Suite No.6 in D
  BWV1012
*Chaconne* from Partita No.2 in D minor
  for Violin BWV 1004

**Side 2**
*Fugue in A minor* from Fugue in G minor
  for Lute
*Gavotte* from Partita No. 3 in E for Violin
  BWV 1006
*Prelude in D minor* from Prelude in C minor
  for Lute BWV 999
*Courante* from 'Cello Suite No.3 in C BWV
  1009
*Sarabande and Bourrée* from Lute Suite No. 1
  in E minor BWV 996
  re-issued 1975

## An Andrés Segovia Recital
DL 9633
Brunswick AXTL 1005
**Side 1**
*Romanesca* A. Mudarra
*Prelude, Ballet, Gigue* S.L. Weiss
*Prelude and Gavotte* J.S. Bach
*Allegro* F. Sor

**Side 2**
*Song Without Words Op.19 No.6* F.
  Mendelssohn
*Minuet from 'Fantasy' Sonata* F. Schubert
*Sonatina in A* F. Moreno Torroba
*Leyenda* I. Albéniz

## An Andrés Segovia Concert
DL 9638
Brunswick AXTL 1010
**Side 1**
*Fantasia* L. Milán
*Suite* R. de Visée
  Prelude, Allemande, Bourrée, Sarabande,
  Gavotte, Gigue,
*Variations on a Theme by Mozart Op.9* F. Sor

**Side 2**
*Allegretto grazioso* G.F. Handel
*Gavotte* G.F. Handel
*Bourrée* J.S. Bach
*Courante* J.S. Bach
*Sonata* M. Giuliani
*Homenaje 'Pour le Tombeau de Debussy'* M. de
  Falla
*Étude* H. Villa-Lobos

## An Andrés Segovia programme
DL 9647
Brunswick AXTL 1060
**Side 1**
*Pavana* L. Milán
*Sarabande & Minuet* G.F. Handel
*Ballet Music from 'Orfeo'* C.W. Gluck
*Sicilienne & Bourrée* J.S. Bach

**Side 2**
*Minuet* F. Sor
*Prelude in A* F. Chopin
*Romanza* R. Schumann
*Andantino variato* Paganini/Ponce
*Waltz in B flat* J. Brahms
*Madroños* F. Moreno Torroba
*Prelude* H. Villa-Lobos

## An Evening With Andrés Segovia
DL 9733
Brunswick AXTL 1070

**Side 1**
*Aria and Corrente* G. Frescobaldi
  (transcribed Segovia)

*Capriccio Diabolico* M. Castelnuovo-Tedesco
*Six Preludes* M. Ponce

**Side 2**
*Minuet* J. Ph. Rameau (transcribed
Segovia)
*Cavatina Suite* A. Tansman
Preludio, Sarabande, Scherzino,
Barcarola, Danza pomposa
*Nocturno* F. Moreno Torroba

## Andrés Segovia
DL 9734
Brunswick AXA 4504
**Side 1**
*Passacaglia* F. Couperin (transcribed
Segovia)
*Prelude* S.L. Weiss
*Allemande* S.L. Weiss
*Minuet* J. Haydn (transcribed Segovia)
*Melodie* E. Grieg (transcribed Segovia)
*Mexican Folk Song* M. Ponce (transcribed
Segovia)
*Serenata Burlesca* F. Moreno Torroba

**Side 2**
*Siciliana* C.P.E. Bach (transcribed Segovia)
*Preludio* C. Franck (transcribed Segovia)
*Allegretto* C. Franck (transcribed Segovia)
*Theme, Variations and Finale* M. Ponce
*Canción* J. Aguirre (transcribed Segovia)
*Guitarreo* C. Pedrell
*Serenade* J. Malats (transcribed Segovia)

## Segovia
## Bach: Chaconne
DL 9751
Brunswick AXTL 1069
**Side 1**
*Prelude*
*Gavotte*        } J.S. Bach
*Chaconne*       } (transcribed Segovia)
*Loure*

**Side 2**
*Minuet in C*
*Andantino*   } F. Sor
*Minuet in D*
*Canzonetta* F. Mendelssohn
*Prelude* H. Villa-Lobos
*Sarabanda* J. Rodrigo

## The Art of Andrés Segovia
Decca DL 9795
**Side 1**
*Six Pieces for Lute* Anonymous
*Fugue* J.S. Bach
*Sonata No.3* M. Ponce

**Side 2**
*Valse* M. Ponce

*Mazurka* M. Ponce
*Homage to Aguirre* (Norteña) J. Gomez
Crespo
*Sardaña* G. Cassadó
*Dance from Venezuela* A. Lauro
*Tonadilla on the Name of Andrés Segovia*
M. Castelnuovo-Tedesco

## Andrés Segovia with the Strings of the Quintetto Chigiana
Decca DL 9832
**Side 1**
*Quintet for Guitar and String Quartet* Op.143
M. Castelnuovo-Tedesco
1. Allegro vivo e schietto
2. Andante mesto
3. Scherzo — Allegro con spirito alla
Marcia
4. Finale — Allegro con fuoco

**Side 2**
*Alba and Postlude* H. Haug
*El Mestre* arr. M. Llobet
*Prelude* A. Scriabin
*Study No.1* H. Villa-Lobos
*Study No.8* H. Villa-Lobos

## Andrés Segovia
## International Classics
MCA MACS 2359
**Side 1**
*Pavana* L. Milán
*Sarabande and Minuet* G.F. Handel
*Ballet* C.W. Gluck
*Sicilienne and Bourrée* J.S. Bach

**Side 2**
*Minuet* F. Sor
*Prelude in A* F. Chopin
*Romanza* R. Schumann
*Andantino Variato* N. Paganini / M. Ponce
*Waltz* J. Brahms
*Madroños* F. Moreno Torroba
*Prelude* H. Villa-Lobos
re-issued 1970

## Andrés Segovia
## Golden Jubilee
Volume 1
DXJ 148
Brunswick AXTL 1088
**Side 1**
*Concierto del Sur* M. Ponce
with The Symphony of the Air
Conductor: Enrique Jordá
I   Allegretto
II  Andante
III Allegro moderato e festivo

123

**Side 2**
*Fantasia para un gentilhombre* J. Rodrigo
with The Symphony of the Air
Conductor: Enrique Jordá
Villano
Ricercare
La Españoleta — Toques de la Caballería
de Napoles
Danza de las Hachas
Canario
1959

## Andrés Segovia
## Golden Jubilee Album
Volume 2
Brunswick AXTL 1089

**Side 1**
*Prelude* S.L. Weiss/M. Ponce
*Pièces caractéristiques* F. Moreno Torroba
Preambulo, Oliveras, Canción, Albada,
Los Mayos, Panorama
*Antaño* O. Esplá
*Allegro in A* M. Ponce

**Side 2**
*The Old Castle* (from 'Pictures at an
Exhibition') M. Mussorgsky
*Segovia* A. Roussel
*Study* A. Segovia
*Canzonetta* ⎫
*Alla Polacca* ⎬ A. Tansman
*Berceuse d'Orient* ⎭
*Tonadilla* E. Granados arr. M. Llobet

## Andrés Segovia
## Golden Jubilee Album
Volume 3 Brunswick AXTL 1090

**Side 1**
*Prelude and Allegro* S. de Murcia
*Study No.1 in C* F. Sor
*Study No.9 in A minor* F. Sor
*Sonata 'Homage to Boccherini'*
M. Castelnuovo-Tedesco
  I   Allegro con spirito
  II  Andantino quasi canzone
  III  Tempo di Minuetto
  IV  Vivo ed energico
*Fandango* J. Rodrigo

**Side 2**
*Passacaglia* L. Roncalli
*Gigue* L. Roncalli
*Gavotta* L. Roncalli
*Study No.20 in C* F. Sor
*Two Minuets* F. Sor
*Danza* E. Granados

## Segovia Plays Boccherini-
## Cassadó and Bach
MCA MUCS 125

124

**Side 1**
*Concerto for Guitar and Orchestra in E*
Boccherini-Cassadó with The Symphony of
the Air Orchestra
Conductor: Enrique Jordá

**Side 2**
*Suite No.3 in A* J.S. Bach (arr. J.W. Duarte)
Prelude, Allemande, Courante,
Sarabande, Bourrée I & Bourrée II,
Gigue
1961

## Andrés Segovia interprète
## Les Européens
MCA MACS 6126

**Side 1**
*Castles of Spain* F. Moreno Torroba
  1.  Turegano
  2.  Torija
  3.  Manzanares del Real
  4.  Montemayor
  5.  Alcaniz
  6.  Siguenza
  7.  Alba de Tormes
  8.  Alcazar de Segovia
*Chant du Paysan* Op.65 No.2 E. Grieg
*Waltz* Op.12 No.2 E. Grieg

**Side 2**
*Prelude and Allegro* S. de Murcia
*Study No.1 in C* F. Sor
*Study No.9 in A minor* F. Sor
*Sonata 'Hommage à Boccherini'*
M. Castelnuovo-Tedesco
  1.  Allegro con spirito
  2.  Andantino quasi canzone
  3.  Tempo di Minuetto
  4.  Vivo ed energico
*Fandango* J. Rodrigo
1961

## Maestro Segovia
MCA MUCS 105

**Side 1**
*Pavane No.6* L. Milán
*Pavane No.5* L. Milán
*Passacaille* R. de Visée★
*Giga Melancolica* Anon.
*Largo assai* J. Haydn★★
*Menuet* J. Haydn★
*Zambra Granadina* I. Albéniz

**Side 2**
*Gallardas* G. Sanz★
*Españoleta* G. Sanz★
*Sonata L79 (K391)* D. Scarlatti
*Andante largo* F. Sor★

Rondo F. Sor★
Song Without Words Op.30 No.3 F.
  Mendelssohn★
Romance de los Pinos F. Moreno Torroba
★arranged Segovia
★★arranged Tárrega
1965

## Segovia
Decca DA 130

**Side 1**
Suite in Modo Polonico A. Tansman
  I   Branle
  II  Gaillarde
  III Kujawiak
  IV  Polonaise
  V   Kolysanka No.1
  VI  Mazurka
  VII Reverie
  VIII Alla Polacca
  IX  Kolysanka No.2
  X   Oberek

**Side 2**
Suite Compostellana F. Mompou
  1. Preludio
  2. Coral
  3. Cuna
  4. Recitativo
  5. Canción
  6. Muñeira
Two Miniatures M. Esteban de Valera
  I  Nana
  II Intermezzo
1966

## Andrés Segovia Interprète Les Italiens
MCA MACS 6123

**Side 1**
Quintet for Guitar and String Quartet Op.143
  M. Castelnuovo-Tedesco
  1. Allegro vivo e schietto
  2. Andante mesto
  3. Scherzo — Allegro con spirito alla
     Marcia
  4. Finale — Allegro con fuoco

**Side 2**
Corrente G. Frescobaldi
Gigue and Gavotte L. Roncalli
Preambulo and Gavotte A. Scarlatti/M. Ponce
Sonata in E minor L352 (K11) ⎫
Sonata in G L79 (K391)        ⎬ D. Scarlatti
Andrés Segovia — guitar       ⎭
Chigiano Quartet:
Riccardo Brengola, Mario Benvenuti —
violins
Giovanni Leone — viola

Lino Filippini — violoncello
1967

## Segovia on Stage
MCA MACS 1032

**Side 1**
Prelude
Minuet  ⎫ H. Purcell
Irish Tune ⎬ (transcribed Segovia)
Jig     ⎭
Rondo
Sonata in A L483 (K322) D. Scarlatti
  (transcribed J. Williams)
Sonata in D minor★ ⎫ G.F. Handel
Fughetta           ⎬ (transcribed Segovia)
Menuet             ⎭
Air★
Passepied★
★  from the Aylesford pieces

**Side 2**
Sarabande ⎫ J.S. Bach
Bourrée   ⎬ (transcribed Segovia)
Double from Suite in B minor for Violin
English Suite Op.31 J.W. Duarte
  Prelude
  Folk Song
  Round Dance
Preambulo and Sardano G. Cassadó
1967

## Mexicana Segovia
MCA MUC 100 (mono)
MCA MUCS 100 (stereo)

**Side 1**
Sonata Mexicana M. Ponce
  I   Allegro moderato
  II  Andantino affetuoso
  III Intermezzo: Allegretto in tempo di
      Serenata
  IV  Allegretto, un poco vivace
Romanza N. Paganini
Sevillana (Fantasia) J. Turina

**Side 2**
Minuet in E Op.32 F. Sor
Minuet in G F. Sor
Minuet in E Op.11 No.10 F. Sor
Sonata Clásica (Hommage à Fernando Sor)
  M. Ponce
  I   Allegro
  II  Andante
  III Menuet
  IV  Allegro
1967

125

## Recital Andrés Segovia
MCA M24.018 Volume 1

**Side 1**
*Granada* I. Albéniz
*Tonadilla* E. Granados (arr. Segovia)
*Danza Española No.10 in G* E. Granados
*Torre Bermeja* I. Albéniz
*Danza Española No.5 in E minor* E. Granados
*Sevilla* I. Albeniz

**Side 2**
*Three Pavanas* L. Milán
*Two Renaissance Pieces* arr. O. Chilesotti
  Se io m'accorgo
  Saltarello
*Burgalesa y Albada* F. Moreno Torroba
*Two Catalan Folksongs* arr. M. Llobet
  El Noi de la Mare
  El Testament d'Amelia
*Damza Mora y Minueto* F. Tárrega
*Prelude; Gigue* ⎫
*Bourrée; Minuet* ⎬ R. de Visée
1969 ⎭

## Segovia Granada
MCA MACS 1968

**Side 1**
*Eight Lessons for Guitar* D. Aguado
*Four Studies for Guitar* F. Sor

**Side 2**
*Canción* M. Ponce
*Canción y Paisaje* M. Ponce
*Granada* I. Albéniz
*Mazurka* A. Tansman
*Spanish Dance in E minor* E. Granados
1970

## Segovia and the Guitar
MCA MACS 1964

**Side 1**
*Canción del Emperador* L. de Narváez
  (sobre 'Mille Regretz' de Josquin)
*Variations on 'Guárdame las Vacas'* L. de
  Narváez
*Two Pieces for Lute:* J. Dowland
  Song and Galliard
*Preambulo and Gavota* A. Scarlatti/Ponce
*Sonata L352 (K11)* D. Scarlatti
*Dos Impresiones Levantinas* O. Espla

**Side 2**
*Fantasia-Sonata* J. Manén
1970

## Andrés Segovia
## Cinco Piezas De "Platero y Yo"
MCA S 26.036

**Side 1**
*Five pieces from 'Platero and I'*

M. Castelnuovo–Tedesco
  I   Platero
  II  Melancolía
  III Angelus
  IV  Golondrinas
  V   La Arrulladora

**Side 2**
*Passacaglia* G. Frescobaldi
*Corrente* G. Frescobaldi
*Fantasia* S.L. Weiss
*Estudio No.3* F. Sor
*Estudio No.17* F. Sor
*Dolor* P. Donostia
*Preludio 'La fille aux cheveux de lin'*
  C. Debussy
1970

## Andrés Segovia
## Castillos de España
MCA S 26.073

**Side 1**
*Castillos de España* F. Moreno Torroba
  I    Turégano
  II   Torija
  III  Manzanares el Real
  IV   Montemayor
  V    Alcañiz
  VI   Sigüenza
  VII  Alba de Tormes
  VIII Alcázar de Segovia
*Canto de Paisano* E. Grieg
*Vals Op.12 No.2* E. Grieg

**Side 2**
*Song and Galliard* J. Dowland
*Melancholy Galliard* J. Dowland
*Allemande: My Lady Hunsdon's Puffe* J.
  Dowland
*Minueto I* ⎱
*Minueto II* ⎰ C.F. Schale
*Tombeau sur la Mort de M. le Comte de Logy*
  S.L. Weiss
*Minueto I* ⎱
*Minueto II* ⎰ S.L. Weiss
1971

## Andrés Segovia
## Sonata Romantica
MCA S 26.087

**Side 1**
*Sonata Romantica* M. Ponce
  I   Allegro Moderato
  II  Andante espressivo
  III Allegretto vivo — piú lento
       espressivo
  IV  Allegro non troppo e serioso

**Side 2**
*Second Series of Pieces from 'Platero y Yo'*
M. Castelnuovo–Tedesco
  I   Retorno

II El Pazo
III El Canario vuela
IV La Primavera
V A Platero en el Cielo de Moguer
1971

## Recuerdos De La Alhambra
### Andrés Segovia
MCA MAC S26091

**Side 1**

*Nine Pieces of Francisco Tárrega*
1. Estudio brillante;  2. Marieta
(Mazurka);  3. Preludio No.5;
4. Preludio No.2;  5. Maria (Gavota);
6. Mazurka in G;  7. Adelita
(Mazurka);  8. Capricho Arabe;
9. Recuerdos de la Alhambra

**Side 2**

*Compositions of Fernando Sor*
1. Introduction and Allegro
2. Two Minuets in A and E major
3. Four Studies
   A major; G major; B minor
   A major
1971

## Andrés Segovia
## The Guitar and I
Volume 1 MCA S 30.020

**Side 1**

*My first years in Granada and Córdoba*
1. Linares (Place of birth)
2. Granada
3. Córdoba
Written and narrated by Andrés Segovia
4. Exercises for developing technique
Introduction and demonstration: Andrés
Segovia

**Side 2**

*Three Studies* N. Coste
  I G minor
  II A minor
  III A major
*Six Studies* F. Sor
  I C major Op.31 No.1
  II A minor Op.35 No.3
  III E major Op.32 No.2
  IV B minor
  V A major Op.35 No.9
  VI D minor Op.35 No.11
*Three Studies* M. Giuliani
  I G major Op.111 No 3
  II A major Op.1 No.11
  III A minor Op.1 No.3
1971

## Andrés Segovia
## The Guitar and I
(Volume 2) Decca DL 710182

**Side 1**

*My first exposure to classic and romantic music*
*Early concerts in Granada and Seville*
*My first concert guitar*
Written and narrated by Andrés Segovia
*Technical formulas*

**Side 2**

*Allegretto in A minor* ⎫
*Larghetto in G*
*Allegretto in G*
*Andantino grazioso in D*  ⎬ M. Giuliani
*Allegretto in C*
*Vivace in A*
*Maestoso in F*
*Allegro in A minor* ⎭
*Allegretto in E* ⎫
*Andantino in D*  ⎬ F. Sor
*Valse in E* ⎭
*Con calma in D minor*
*Allegretto in A minor* N. Coste
*Scherzando in C*
*Study in the form of a Minuet* F. Tárrega
1972

## Andrés Segovia
## Obras Breves Españolas
Movieplay 17.0511/0

**Side 1**

*Diferencias sobre 'Guárdame las Vacas'* L. de
  Narváez
*Sonata in D* E. de Valderrábano
*Pavana in E minor* D. Pisador
*Gallarda in D* A. Mudarra
*Folias de España* Op.15: F. Sor
  Theme and Four Variations
*Two Catalan Folk Songs:* arr. M. Llobet
  El Mestre
  La Filla del Marxant
*Capricho Arabe* F. Tárrega

**Side 2**

*Fandanguillo* F. Moreno Torroba
*Arada* F. Moreno Torroba
*Albada* F. Moreno Torroba
*Nocturno* F. Moreno Torroba
*Burgalesa* F. Moreno Torroba
*Allegretto from Sonatina in A* F. Moreno
  Torroba
*Torre Bermeja* I. Albéniz
1973

127

**Andrés Segovia**
**Recital Intimo**
Intercord INT 160.808

**Side 1**
Bourrée S.L. Weiss (arr. A. Segovia)
Sonatina in D G. Benda (arr. A. Segovia)
Sonatina in D minor G. Benda (arr. A.
  Segovia)
Prelude; Sarabande J.S. Bach (arr. J.W.
  Duarte)
Menuett. I & II J.S. Bach (arr. J.W. Duarte)
  from 'Cello Suite No.1
Larghetto D. Scarlatti (arr. J.W. Duarte)
Menuett D. Scarlatti (arr. J.W. Duarte)

**Side 2**
Andante Largo in C minor & Menuett in C
  F. Sor
Menuett in A F. Sor
Menuett in C F. Sor
Dipso V. Asencio
Prelude in E M. Ponce
1973

**Segovia**
MCA 410 031
Volume 1

**Side 1**
Sonata in D minor ⎫
Fughetta            ⎪ G.F. Handel
Minuet              ⎬ (transcribed Segovia)
Air                 ⎪
Passepied           ⎭
Prelude             ⎫
Minuet              ⎪ H. Purcell
A New Irish Tune    ⎬ (transcribed Segovia)
Jig                 ⎪
Rondo               ⎭
Passacaille R. de Visée
Gigue mélancholie Anonymous

**Side 2**
Suite No. 3 in A J.S. Bach arr. J.W. Duarte
  1. Prelude;  2. Allemande;
  3. Courante;  4. Sarabande;
  5. Bourrée I; Bourrée II; 6. Gigue
issued 1974

**Segovia**
Volume 2 MCA 410 032

**Side 1**
Pavane No.6 ⎱ L. Milán
Pavane No.5 ⎰
Gallardas   ⎱ G. Sanz
Españoleta  ⎰

128

Sarabande ⎱ G.F. Handel
Minuet    ⎰ transcribed Segovia
Sicilienne ⎱
Bourrée    ⎰ J.S. Bach

**Side 2**
Eight Pieces for Guitar D. Aguado
Four Studies F. Sor
  1.  Study No.10
  2.  Study No.15
  3.  Study No.19
  4.  Study No.6
issued 1974

**Segovia**
Volume 3 MCA 410 033

**Side 1**
Concierto del Sur M. Ponce
  1.  Allegretto
  2.  Andante
  3.  Allegro moderato e festivo
Orchestra of the Symphony of the Air
Conductor: Enrique Jordá

**Side 2**
Minuet in E Op.32 ⎱ F. Sor
Minuet in G        ⎰
Minuet in E Op.11 No.10
Sonata clásica M. Ponce
  1.  Allegro
  2.  Andante
  3.  Menuet
  4.  Allegro
issued 1974

**Segovia**
Volume 4 MCA 410 034

**Side 1**
Fantasia por un Gentilhombre J. Rodrigo
  1.  Villano
  2.  Ricercare
  3.  Españoleta
  4.  Danza de las Hachas
  5.  Canarios
Orchestra of the Symphony of the Air
Conductor: Enrique Jordá

**Side 2**
Study No.1 H. Villa-Lobos
Homage to Aguirre J. Gomez Crespo
Valse M. Ponce
Albada F. Moreno Torroba
Allegro from Sonatina F. Moreno Torroba
Sevillana (Fantasia) J. Turina
issued 1974

**Segovia**
Volume 5 MCA 410 035

**Side 1**
Tonadilla E. Granados
Danza No.10 in G E. Granados

*Leyenda* I. Albéniz
*Zambra Granadina* I. Albéniz

**Side 2**
*Canción* M. Ponce
*Canción y Paisaje* M. Ponce
*Granada* I. Albéniz
*Danza No.5 in E minor* E. Granados
*Allegretto un poco vivace* M. Ponce
(Fourth movement of Sonata Mexicana)
issued 1974

**Andrés Segovia**
**The Intimate Guitar /2**
RCA Red Seal ARL1 1323 stereo

**Side 1**
*The Anna Magdalena Notebook:* J.S. Bach
transcribed Segovia
Menuet I, Menuet II, Marche I, Menuet
III, Marche II, Menuet IV, Musette
*Sicilienne in D minor* F. Sor
*Introduction and Variations on
'Malbrough s'en va-t-en guerre'* F. Sor

**Side 2**
*Variations on a Theme* J.M. Molleda
*Preludios Vascos: Dolor* San Sebastián
(transcribed Segovia)
*Capricho Catalan* I. Albéniz
*Serenade* G. Samazeuilh
1976

**Reveries**
**Andrés Segovia**
RCA Red Seal RL 12602

**Side 1**
*Ballet (Dance of the Blessed Spirits) from
'Orfeo'* C.W. Gluck
*Album for the Young* Op.68 R. Schumann,
transcribed Segovia
No.26
No.1 Melody
No.16 First Loss
No.5 Little Piece
No.2 Soldier's March
No.9 Little Folk Song
No.6 The Poor Orphan
No.10 The Merry Peasant
*Rêverie* (Träumerei) R. Schumann, trans-
scribed Segovia (No.7 from 'Scenes from
Childhood' Op. 15)
*Romanza* R. Schumann, transcribed
Segovia

**Side 2**
*Mystic Suite* V. Asencio
Getsemani
Dipso
Pentecostes
*Ronsard* (from 'Platero and I')
M. Castelnuovo-Tedesco
*Castellana* F. Moreno Torroba
1978

## COMPOSERS RECORDED BY SEGOVIA

**Luys Milán**
*Fantasia XVI* Decca DL 9638
*Pavana* Decca DL 9647
*Pavanas Nos.5,6* Decca DL 710039
*Pavanas Nos.6,5* MUCS 105
*Six Pavanas* Decca DL 710167
*Three Pavanas* (78/10'') 710/40.075 (1949);
Decca DL 8022; M 24018

**Alonso Mudarra**
*Romanesca* Decca DL 9633

**Luys de Narváez**
*Canción del Emperador* Decca DL 9931; Decca
DL 79931 (stereo)
*Diferencias sobre 'Guardame las Vacas'* Decca
DL 9931; Decca DL 79931 (stereo)

**Vincenzo Galilei** 1520–1591
*Miscellaneous Pieces:* Decca DL 8022; Decca
Album 710/40.075 (1949); Decca DL 9795

**John Dowland** 1563–1625
*Captain Digorie Piper's Galliard* MCA
S/26.073; Decca DL 710171
*Melancholy Galliard* MCA S/26.073; Decca
DL 710171
*My Lady Hunsdon's Puffe* MCA S/26.073;
Decca DL 710171

**Girolamo Frescobaldi** 1583–1643
*Aria con Variazioni detta La Frescobalda*
Decca DL 9733
*Corrente* Decca DL 710054
*Passacaglia* Decca DL 710054

**Gaspar Sanz** 1640–1710
*Gallardas & Españoleta:* Decca DL 710039

**Henry Purcell** 1658–1695
*Miscellaneous Pieces* Decca DL 710110

**Ludovico Roncalli**
*Gigue & Gavotte* MCA MACS 6123; AXTL
1090
*Passacaglia* AXTL 1090

129

**Robert de Visée** c1660–1725
*Suite in D minor* Decca DL 9638
*Suites & Miscellaneous Pieces:* Decca
  710/40.078 (1949); Decca DL 8022; Decca
  DL 710039; AXTL 1010; MUCS 105; MCA
  M/24.O18

**Johann Sebastian Bach** 1685–1750
*Allemande* (1st Lute Suite) HMV D 1536;
  Decca DL 710167
*Bourrée* (1st Lute Suite) Saga XID 5248;
  Heliodor HS 25010; SQN 101
*Bourrée* (3rd 'Cello Suite) Decca DL 9647;
  Decca DL 9751
*Bourrée* (from Suite in B minor for
  Unaccompanied Violin) Decca DL 710140;
  MACS 1032; AXTL 1010
*'Cello Suite No.3* (arr. John W. Duarte):
  MUCS 125; MCA 410031
*Chaconne* MGM E3015/M2306 (1953); RCA
  1442A (1952); Heliodor HS 25010; Everest
  EV 3251E; Saga 5248; AXTL 1069
*Courante* (3rd 'Cello Suite) HMV 475;
  Victrola 1298; MGM E123; RCA 1442A
  (1952); MGM E3015/M2306 (1953); Everest
  EV 3251 E; SQN 101; AXTL 1010
*Fugue in A minor* Heliodor HS 25010; MGM
  E3015/M2306 (1953); MGM E123; Saga 5248;
  Decca DL 9795
*Gavotte* (4th Lute Suite) HMV D1255 (1927);
  Victor Red Seal 6766; Decca DL 9751;
  Everest EV 3251 E
*Gavotte* (6th 'Cello Suite) AXTL 1005
*Gavottes 1 & 2* (6th 'Cello Suite) Everest
  EV 3251 E; SQN 101
*Gigue* (2nd Lute Suite) Decca DL 710167
*Prelude* (1st 'Cello Suite) AXTL 1005
*Prelude in D minor* Decca DL 9751; Saga 5248
*Sarabande* (1st Lute Suite) Saga XID 5248;
  Heliodor HS 25010; SQN 101
*Sarabande* (2nd Lute Suite) Decca DL 710167
*Sarabande, Bourrée, Double* (from Suite in B
  minor for Unaccompanied Violin) Decca
  DL 710140; MACS 1032

**François Couperin** (1668–1733)
*Passacaglia* Decca DL 9734

**Santiago de Murcia**
*Prelude y Allegro* Decca DL 710034

**Jean Philippe Rameau** 1683–1764
*Minuet* Decca A596 (1947); Decca DL 9733;
  AXTL 1070

**Domenico Scarlatti** 1685–1757
*Sonatas*
*L352 (K11)* Decca A596 (1947); Decca ED
  3503; MCA 3070
*L79 (K391) L483 (K322);* Decca DL
  710140; RCA ARLI 0865

**George Frederick Handel** 1685–1759
*Aylesford Pieces* Decca DL 710140
*Sarabande and Variations* Decca DL 9647
*Various Pieces* Decca DL 9638

**Sylvius Leopold Weiss** 1686–1750
*Fantasia* Decca DL 710054
*Tombeau sur la Mort de M. le Comte de
  Logy* Decca DL 710171

**Christian Friedrich Schale** 1713–1800
*Minuets I & II* Decca DL 710171

**Georg Benda** 1722–1795
*Two Sonatas* RCA ARLI 0865

**Josef Haydn** 1732–1809
*Largo & Minuet* Decca DL 710039
*Minuet* Decca DL 9734

**Luigi Boccherini** 1743–1805
*Concerto* (arr. Cassadó) Decca DL 710043

**Fernando Sor** 1778–1839
*Andante Largo* Op.5 No.5 Decca DL 710039
*Introduction & Allegro* Op.14 Decca DL 9794
*Largo from Fantasia* Op.7 ARLI 0865
*Minuet in C* Decca DL 9647
*Minuets in C, D* Decca DL 9751
*Minuets in A, E* Decca DL 9794
*Minuets in E,G,E* Decca DL 710145
*Minuets in A, C* RCA ARLI 0865
*Rondo* from Op.22 Decca DL 710039
*Sonata: Allegro* from Op.25 Decca DL 9633
*Studies Nos. 1,9,20* Decca DL 710034
*Studies Nos. 3,17* Decca DL 710054
*Studies Nos. 6, 10, 15, 29* Decca DL 710063
*Studies Nos. 5,12,14,16* Decca DL 9794
*Studies:* Op.31 No.1; Op.32 No.2; Op.35
  Nos.3,9,11,22 Decca DL 710179
*Variations on Folies d'Espagne* Op.15a RCA
  ARLI 0485
*Variations on 'Malbrough'* Op.28 RCA ARLI
  1323
*Variations on a Theme of Mozart* Op.9 HMV
  D 1255 (1927); Decca DL 9638

**Mauro Giuliani** 1781–1829
*Allegro from Sonata* Op.15 AXTL 1010
*Eight Little Pieces* Decca DL 710182
*Three Studies* Decca DL 710179

**Niccolo Paganini** 1782–1840
*Andante variato* (arr. Ponce) from Grand
  Sonata in A Decca DL 9647
*Romanza* Decca A596 (1947)

**Dionisio Aguado** 1784–1849
*Eight Lessons* Decca DL 710063

**Franz Schubert** 1797–1828
*Minuet* Op.78 (D894) AXTL 1005

**Felix Mendelssohn** 1809–1847
*Canzonetta* AXTL 1069
*Songs Without Words* Decca DL 9633; MUCS
  105

130

**Frédéric François Chopin** 1810–1849
*Prelude in A* Decca DL 9647

**Robert Schumann** 1810–1856
*Album for the Young* RCA RL 12602
*Romanza* RCA RL 12602; AXTL 1060
*Träumerei* RCA RL 12602

**Jean Alard** 1815–1888
*Study in A* (arr. Tárrega) Decca DL 9794;
MCA S26091

**Modest Petrovich Mussorgsky**
1839–1881
*The Old Castle* from 'Pictures at an
Exhibition' Brunswick AXTL 1089

**Francisco Tárrega** 1852–1909
*Adelita* Decca DL 9794; MCA S26091
*Capricho Arabe* Decca DL 9794; MCA
S26091
*Danza Mora* Decca 710/40077 (1949), DL
8022
*Maria* Decca DL 9794; MCA S26091
*Marieta* Decca DL 9794; MCA S26091
*Mazurka in G* Decca DL 9794; MCA
S26091
*Minuet* Decca 710/40077 (1949); Decca DL
8022
*Preludes Nos.2&5* Decca DL 9794
*Recuerdos de la Alhambra* HMV D1305
(1927); Decca DL 9794; MCA S26091

**Isaac Albéniz** (1860–1909)
*Asturias (Leyenda)* Decca DL 9633; Decca
DL 710160; AXTL 1005
*Capricho Catalan* ARLI 1323
*Granada* Decca 3824/29.154 (USA 1945);
ED 3510 Vol.II; A 384; DL 8022; DU 707
(1949); DL 710063; MACS 1968; MCA
M–24.018
*Mallorca* Decca DL 710167
*Sevilla* Decca 384/29.156 (USA 1945);
ED 3503 Vol. I; A 384; DL 8022; DU 707
(1949); DL 710160; MCA M–24.018
*Torre Bermeja* Decca 384/29.155 (USA
1945); A 384, DL 8022; DU 707 (1949);
RCA ARLI 0485; MCA M–24.018
*Zambra Granadina* Decca DL 710039;
MUCS 105

**Enrique Granados** 1867–1916
*La Maja de Goya* Decca 384/29.154 (1945);
A 384; Decca DL 710046; Decca DL
710160; Decca DL 8022; MCA M24018;
AXTL 1089
*Spanish Dances* Op.37
No.5 Decca 384/29.156 (1945); ED
3503; Decca DL 710063
No.10 ED 3510; Decca DL 710034; Decca
DL 710160
Nos. 5 & 10 A384; Decca DL 8022; MCA
M24018

**Albert Roussel** 1869–1937
*Segovia* Op.29 Decca DL 710046

**Joaquín Malats** 1872–1912
*Serenata Española* Decca DL 9734

**Alexander Nikolaievich Scriabin**
1872–1915
*Prelude* Decca DL 9832

**Manuel de Falla** 1876–1946
*Homenaje — Pour le tombeau de Debussy*
Decca DL 9638

**Miguel Llobet** 1878–1938
Catalan Folk Songs
*El Mestre* Decca DL 9832
*El Noy de la Mare* Decca 710/40.077
(1949); Decca DL 8022; MCA M24018
*El Testament d'Amelia* Decca 710/40.077
(1949); Decca DL 8022; MCA M24018

**Manuel Ponce** 1882–1948
*Concierto del Sur* Decca DL 710027; DXL
148; Decca DL 9995/6/7; HOF 522; MCA
410033
*Mazurka* HMV DA 1552; Decca DL 9795

Pastiches:
*Gavotte & Sarabande* (A. Scarlatti) Decca
596/24.147 (1949); ED 3510
*Prelude* (Weiss) Decca DL 710046
*Prelude, Allemande* (Weiss) Decca DL 9734
*Prelude, Allemande, Gigue* (Weiss) HMV DB
1565
*Prelude, Ballet, Gigue* (Weiss) Decca DL
9633
*Sarabande & Gavotte* (Weiss) HMV DA 1225

Preludes:
*Prelude in E* ARL 10865
*Six Preludes* AXTL 1070
*Rondo on a Theme by Sor* ML 4732

Sonatas:
*Allegro* (Sonata Mexicana) HMV AB 656;
Decca DL 710046
*Campo* (Sonatina Meridional) Decca DL
710063; MCA 410034
*Rondo* (Sonata Clásica) Columbia LB 130
(1951)
*Sonata Clásica* Decca DL 710145
*Sonata Mexicana* Decca DL 710145
*Sonata No. 3* Decca DL 9795
*Sonata Romántica* Decca DL 710093
*Sonatina Meridional* ML 4732

*Thème varié et Finale* Decca DL 9734
*Tres Canciónes populares mexicanas* Decca
DL 9734; Decca DL 710063
*Valse* HMV DA 1552; Decca DL 9795;
Decca DL 710160; MCA 410034
*Variations on 'Folia de España' and Fugue*
HMV DB 1567/8

131

**Joaquín Turina** 1882–1949
*Fandanguillo* Op.36 HMV D 1305; Victor
    Red Seal 6767; CAX 10569; LX 1248;
    HLM 7134
*Sevillana* (Fantasia) Op.29 Decca DL
    710145; Decca DL 710160; MCA 410034

**Joan Manén** 1883–1971
*Fantasia-Sonata* MCA MACS 1964

**Oscar Esplá** 1886–1976
*Antaño* Decca DL 710046
*Two Danzas Levantinas* Decca DL 9931

**Heitor Villa-Lobos** 1887–1959
*Prelude No.1* Decca DL 9647; Decca DL
    710167
*Prelude No.3* Decca DL 9751
*Study No.1* Decca DL 710160; MCA
    410034
*Study Nos. 1 & 8* Columbia LX 1248
    (1949); HLM 7134; Decca DL 9832
*Study No.7* Decca DL 7638

**Federico Moreno Torroba** 1891–1982
*Burgalesa* Decca 710–40.076 (USA 1949);
    Decca DL 8022; ARLI D485
*Castellana* RL 12602
*Castillos de España* Decca DL 710171; MCA
    S26073
*Madroños* Decca DL 9467
*Nocturno* HMV E569; Decca DL 9733;
    ARLI D485; AXTL 1070
*Pièces caractéristiques* (complete) Decca DL
    710046; DXL 148; Decca DL 9995/6/7
*Albada* Decca 710–40.076(USA 1949);
    Decca DL 8022; Decca DL 710160; MCA
    410034
*Romance de los Pinos* Decca DL 710039
*Serenata Burlesca* Decca DL 9734
*Sonatina in A* HMV E 475; Victrola 1298;
    Decca DL 9633
*Allegretto* ARLI 0485
*Allegro* MCA 410134; Decca DL 710160
*Suite Castellana*:
    Arada Decca 710–40.076 (USA 1949)
    Arada, Danza Columbia LX 1248 (1950);
    Columbia ML 4732
    Arada, Fandanguillo CAX 10568; Decca
    DL 8022; ARLI 0485; HLM 7134 (1978)
*Fandanguillo* Columbia LX 1248 (1950)
*Fandanguillo, Preludio* HMV E 526; Victor
    Red Seal 1487

**Federico Mompou** b. 1893
*Suite Compostellana* DA 130

**Andrés Segovia** b. 1893
*Estudio sin Luz* AXTL 1089

**Mario Castelnuovo-Tedesco** 1895–1968
*Capriccio Diabolico* Op.8 (Omaggio a
    Paganini) Decca DL 9733; AXTL 1070
*Concerto in D* Op.99 Columbia LX 1404/5/
    6(1949); Columbia ML 4732; Odeon
    33QCX 127; HOF 522; HLM 7134
*Platero y Yo* (5 Pieces from) Decca DL
    710054; MCA S26036; MCA S26087
*Ronsard* RL 12602
*Quintet* Op.143 Decca DL 9832
*Sonata in D* Op.77 (Omaggio a Boccherini)
    Decca DL 710034; DXL 148; Decca DL
    9995–7
*4th Movement* HMV DB 3243
*Tarantella* Columbia LX 1229 (1949);
    HLM 7134
*Tonadilla on the name Andrés Segovia* Decca
    DL 9795

**Alexandre Tansman** b. 1897
*Cavatina* (Suite) Decca DL 9733
*In Modo Polonico* DA 130; Decca DL 710112
*Mazurka* Decca DL 710063
*3 Pieces* Decca DL 710046; DXL 148
*Prelude* Decca DL 710167

**Jorge Gomez Crespo**
*Norteña* LB 130 (1949); HLM 7134; Odeon
    33QCX 127; Decca DL 9795

**Hans Haug** 1900–1967
*Alba & Postlude* Decca DL 9832

**Joaquín Rodrigo** b. 1901
*Fandango* Decca DL 710034
*Fantasia para un Gentilhombre* DXL 148;
    Decca DL 9995/6/7; MCA 410034
*Zarabanda Lejana* Decca DL 9751

**Vicente Asencio** b. 1903
*Mystic Suite* RL 12602 (1977)

**Albert Harris** b. 1916
*Variations and Fugue on a Theme of Handel*
    Decca DL 710167

**John W. Duarte** b. 1919
*English Suite* Op.31 MACS 1032

132

# 14
# *SEGOVIA EDITIONS*

The following list, in alphabetical order, consists of editions of music involving Andrés Segovia. In most instances his work concerned either the complete transcribing and editing of compositions from earlier periods of history or the preparation of contemporary works dedicated to him (including fingering, editing, correcting of unplayable passages, liaison with publishers, etc) so as to make them available for the widest possible public.

A few of the works listed do not contain detailed editing by Segovia. With the *Douze Études* of Heitor Villa-Lobos, Segovia wrote a preface to the studies dedicated to him but did not affix suitable fingerings. Normally however Segovia's commitment to the task of establishing a publishable text was total and composers who were not guitarists themselves usually preferred his complete guidance in this way.

† dedicated to Andrés Segovia:

Associated Music Publishers Inc., New York
Belwin Mills, New York
Berben, Ancona — Milan
Biblioteca Fortea, Madrid
Celesta Publishing Co., New York
Columbia Music Co., Washington D.C.
Durand & Cie, Paris
Eschig (Max) Éditions, Paris
Huegel & Cie, Paris
Kalmus, New York
Marks (Edward B.) Music Corporation, New York
Peer International Corporation, New York
Ricordi, Buenos Aires & Milan
Salabert Éditions, Paris
Schott Guitar Archives, London & Mainz
Union Musical Española, Madrid

**Julián Aguirre**
*Triste No.4* — Ricordi, Buenos Aires

**Isaac Albéniz**
*Asturias-Leyenda* — Ricordi Buenos Aires
*Granada* — Celesta
*Mallorca* — Celesta
*Oriental* — Celesta
*Tango* — Schott
*Zambra Granadina* — Celesta

**Vicente Asencio**
*Suite mística* (Getsemani — Dipso —
Pentecostes) — Berben

**Carl Philipp Emanuel Bach**
*La Sibylle; Siciliana* — Schott
*La Xénophone* — Schott

**Johann Sebastian Bach**
*Chaconne* — Schott
*Collected Pieces* — Schott

 *Volume I:*
 Prelude, Allemande,
 Minuetto I,
 Minuetto II

 *Volume II:*
 Courante, Gavotte

 *Volume III:*
 Andante, Bourrée,
 Double

*Courante* — Columbia
*Gavotte* — Celesta
*Gavotte* — Schott
*3 Pieces from the Notebook of Anna Magdalena*
 — Schott
*Prelude* — Schott
*Prelude and Fugue* — Schott
*Sarabande* — Celesta
*Sarabande* Schott
*Sarabande* (from Violin Sonata II) — Union
 Musical Española
*Siciliana* (from Violin Sonata I) — Union
 Musical Española

**Ludwig van Beethoven**
*Minuet from Sonata* (Op.31 No.3) — Ricordi,
 Buenos Aires
*Minuet from Sonata* (Op.31 No.3) — Union
 Musical Española

**Vincenzo Bellini**
*Dolenta immagine di fille mia* (for voice and
 guitar) — Schott

**Georg Benda**
*2 Sonatinas* — Schott

**Luigi Boccherini**
*Concerto in E for guitar and orchestra* (Cassadó)
 (piano version) — Schott

**Johannes Brahms**
*Waltz* Op.39 No.8 — Schott
*Waltz* Op.39 No.15 — Columbia

**Alfonso Broqua**
*Milongueos* (Evaciones Criollas)[†] — Eschig

**Mario Castelnuovo-Tedesco**
*Capriccio diabolico* (Omaggia a Paganini[†])
 — Ricordi, Milan
*Concerto in D Op.77 for guitar and orchestra*
 (guitar and piano version)[†] — Schott
*Fantasia for guitar and piano Op.145[†]* —
 Schott
*Naranjos en Flor* — Ricordi
*Quintet Op.143 for guitar and string quartet[†]* —
 Schott
*Rondo Op. 129[†]* — Schott
*Serenade for guitar and chamber orchestra*
 (guitar and piano version)[†] — Schott
*Sonata in D Op. 77* (Omaggio a Boccherini)[†]
 — Schott
*Tarantella* [†] — Ricordi, Milan
*Tonadilla on the name Andrés Segovia[†]* —
 Schott
*Variations à travers les siècles* — Schott

**Frédéric François Chopin**
*Mazurka* Op.63 No.3 — Schott

**Louis Couperin**
*Passacaglia* — Schott

**Jorge Gomez Crespo**
*Norteña* (Homage a Aguirre) — Columbia

**John W. Duarte**
*English Suite[†]* (Prelude — Folk Song —
 Round Dance) — Novello
*Three Modern Miniatures[†]* (Prelude —
 Ostinato — Scherzando) — Schott

**César Franck**
*4 Pieces* — Schott

**Girolamo Frescobaldi**
*Aria con Variazioni detta 'La Frescobalda'*—
 Schott
*5 Pieces:*
 Corrente, Passacaglia, Corrente,
 Gagliarda, Corrente — Schott

**Giuseppe Giordani**
*'Caro mio ben'* (for voice and guitar) —
 Schott

**Christoph Willibald von Gluck**
*Ballet* — Columbia

**Edvard Hagerup Grieg**
*Canto del Campesina* — Union Musical
 Española
*Melody* — Columbia

**George Frederick Handel**
*Air from Suite No.X* — Union Musical
Española
*8 Aylesford Pieces* — Schott

**Albert Harris**
*Variations and Fugue on a Theme of Handel†* —
Schott

**Josef Haydn**
*Minuet* — Ricordi, Buenos Aires
*Minuet from Quartet in G* — Schott
*Minuet* — Union Musical Española

**Johann Kuhnau**
*4 Pieces:* Prelude, Sarabande, Minuet,
Gavotte — Schott

**Paquita Madriguera**
*Humorada* — Columbia

**Joan Manén**
*Fantasia-Sonata†* — Schott

**Felix Mendelssohn**
*Song without Words* Op.19 No.4 — Union
Musical Española
*Song without Words* Op.30 No.3 — Ricordi,
Buenos Aires

**Darius Milhaud**
*Segoviana†* — Huegel & Cie

**J. Munoz Molleda**
*Diferencias sobre un Tema†* — Columbia

**Federico Mompou**
*Suite Compostellana†* — Salabert

**Wolfgang Amadeus Mozart**
*Minuet* — Schott

**Alonso Mudarra**
*Romanesca* — Schott

**Carlos Pedrell**
*Guitarreo†* — Schott
*Lamento†* — Schott
*Página romántica†* — Schott

**Manuel Ponce**
*Andantino variato* (Paganini) — Peer
International Corp. New York
*3 Canciones populares mexicanas†* — Schott
*Concierto del Sur for guitar and orchestra
(guitar and piano version)†* — Peer
International
*Estudio†* — Schott
*Preludes 1_6†* — Schott
*Preludes 7_12†* — Schott
*Preludio†* — Schott
*Sonata III†* — Schott
*Sonata clásica* (Hommage à Fernando Sor)†
– Schott
*Sonata romántica* (Hommage à Franz
Schubert)† — Schott

*Sonatina meridional†* — Schott
*Thème varié et Finale†* — Schott
*Valse†* — Schott
*Variations on "Folia de España" and Fugue†*
— Schott

**Emilio Pujol**
*Homenaje a Tárrega* — Schott

**Henry Purcell**
*Three Pieces:* — Columbia
A New Irish Tune
Jig
Minuet

**Jean Philippe Rameau**
*2 Minuets* — Schott

**Joaquín Rodrigo**
*Fantasia para un Gentilhombre* (for guitar and
orchestra)† — Schott
*Tres piezas españolas* (Fandango — Passacaglia — Zapateado)† — Schott

**Albert Roussel**
*Segovia* Op.29† — Durand

**Gustav Samazeuilh**
*Sérénade†* — Durand

**Alessandro Scarlatti**
*Se Florinda e fedele* for voice and guitar —
Celesta

**Domenico Scarlatti**
*Sonata* — Celesta
*Sonata in A minor* — Schott
*Sonata in E minor* — Schott

**Christian Friedrich Schale**
*2 Minuets* — Schott

**Franz Schubert**
*3 Little Waltzes* — Union Musical Española

**Robert Schumann**
*Album for the Young* Op.68:
*Andante cantabile* — Ricordi, Buenos Aires
*A Little Study* — Ricordi, Buenos Aires
*May, charming May* — Union Musical
Española
*The Merry Peasant* — Ricordi, Buenos Aires
*New Year's Song* — Union Musical Española
*Northern Song* Ricordi, Buenos Aires
*Popular Song* Ricordi, Buenos Aires
*Soldiers' March* Ricordi, Buenos Aires
*Romanza* Columbia
*Scenes from Childhood* Op.15:
The Entreating Child — Schott
Frightening — Schott

**Alexander Scriabin**
*Prelude* Op.16 No.4 — Celesta

**Andrés Segovia**
5 Anecdotes *(i) — Belwin Mills
3 Daily Studies — Schott
  1.  Oración *(ii)
  2.  Remembranza *(iii)
  3.  Divertimento *(iv)
4 Easy Lessons — Celesta
Estudio *(v) — Columbia
Estudio sin luz *(vi) — Schott
Estudio-Vals — Columbia
Impromptu Biblioteca Fortea, Kalmus
Lessons No.11 & 12 — Belwin Mills
Macarena Belwin Mills
2 Pieces: — Belwin Mills
  Giga melancólica
  (Froberger)
  Neblina *(vii)
Prelude in Chords — Celesta
3 Preludios — Biblioteca Fortea, Kalmus
Tonadilla — Biblioteca Fortea, Kalmus
Diatonic Major and Minor Scales — Columbia
Slur Exercises and Chromatic Octaves —
  Columbia

*(i)   recorded by Laurindo Almeida (CTL
   7089)
*(ii)  recorded by Akinobu Matsuda (ZDA
   205) John Williams (ECB 315)
*(iii) recorded by Alirio Diaz (VPD 20002)
*(v)  recorded by John Williams (ECB
   3151)
*(vi)  recorded by Eduardo Abreu (SDD
   219)
      Oscar Caceres (STU 70614)
      Andrés Segovia (AXTL 1089)
*(vii) recorded by Laurindo Almeida (CTL
   7089)

**Reginald Smith Brindle**
Danza Pagana † — Schott
Fuego Fatuo †

**Fernando Sor**
Andante Largo — Ricordi, Buenos Aires
Sonata Op.25 (Allegro) — Ricordi, Buenos
Aires
20 Studies: Edward B. Marks/Belwin Mills
  1.  Op.6 No.8 in C; 2.  Op.35 No.13 in
  C; 3.  Op.6 No.2 in A; 4.  Op.6 No.1
  in D; 5.  Op.35 No.22 in B minor;
  6.  Op.35 No.17 in D; 7.  Op.31 No.21
  in F; 8.  Op.31 No.16 in D minor;
  9.  Op.31 No.20 in A minor;
  10.  Op.31 No.19 in A; 11.  Op.6 No.3
  in E; 12.  Op.6 No.6 in A; 13.  Op.6
  No.9 in D minor; 14.  Op.6 No.12 in A;
  15.  Op.35 No.16 in D minor; 16.Op.29
  No.23 in G; 17.  Op.6 No.11 in E
  minor; 18.  Op.29 No.22 in Eb;
  19.  Op.29 No.13 in Bb; 20.Op.29
  No.17 in C

(The numbering of Studies Op.29 follows
on after the two sets of Studies Op.6. All
three volumes were dedicated to Sor's
pupils.)
Variations on 'O cara armonia' from The
  Magic Flute by Mozart, Op.9 — Schott

**Alexandre Tansman**
I. Canzonetta † — Max Eschig
II. Alla Polacca †
III Berceuse d'Orient †
Cavatina: † — Schott
  Preludio
  Sarabande
  Scherzino
  Barcarola
Danza Pomposa † — Ricordi, Buenos Aires
  Schott
Hommage a Chopin † — Eschig
  1.  Prelude
  2.  Nocturne
  3.  Valse Romantique
Mazurka † — Schott
Suite in Modo Polonica † — Eschig
  Entrée
  Gaillarde
  Kujawiak
  Tempo de Polonaise
  Kolysanka No.1
  Reverie
  Alla Polacca
  Kolysanka No.2
  Oberek

**Federico Moreno Torroba**
Burgalesa † — Schott
Contradanza † — Associated Music
Jota Cervantina † — Associated Music
Madroños † — Associated Music
Nocturno † — Schott
Pièces caractéristiques † — Schott,
  Volume I:
  Préambulo
  Oliveras
  Melodía
Pièces caractéristiques † — Schott
  Volume II:
  Los Mayos
  Albada
  Panorama
Preludio † — Schott
Serenata burlesca † — Ricordi, Buenos
  Aires; Schott
Sonatina in A † — Columbia; Ricordi,
  Buenos Aires
Suite Castellana; † — Ricordi, Buenos Aires;
  Schott
  Fandanguillo
  Arada
  Danza
Vieja Leyenda † — Union Musical Española

**Joaquín Turina**
*Fandanguillo*, Op.36 † — Schott
*Hommage à Tárrega*: Op.69 † — Schott
  Garrotín
  Soleares
*Ráfaga*, Op.53 † — Schott
*Sevillana*, Op.29 † — Columbia; Sociedad
  Musical Daniel
*Sonata*, Op. 61 † — Schott

**Johann Baptiste Vanhall**
*Cantabile* — Schott
*Minuetto* — Schott

**Heitor Villa-Lobos**
*Concerto for guitar and small orchestra* † —
  Eschig
*12 Studies* † — Eschig

**Johann Friedrich Wenkel**
*Musette* — Schott

# 15
# A SELECTION OF RECITAL PROGRAMMES 1936–82

BY THE 1930's Segovia's recitals had acquired much of the shape and repertoire charactistic of more recent years. The programme format, tripartite with a balanced variety selected from several centuries, was not only more ambitious than any previous guitarist's but set a stimulating example for subsequent recitalists. His programmes represent a thorough exploration of the best the repertoire could offer with a minimum of nine composers for each concert, represented by short appetising one movement works as well as substantial sonatas, suites, and sets of variations.

Many features of the structure of a Segovia recital will emerge from close scrutiny of the following, including the significance of transcriptions from other instruments, the importance of J.S. Bach and Albéniz, and the evidence of Segovia's loyalty to the chosen retinue of contemporary composers whose works he most admires.

**The Hague** 27 November 1936
First appearance in Holland
Canzone e saltarello — O. Chilesotti
Pavane et Gaillarde — G Sanz
Preambulo et Gavotta — A. Scarlatti
Gigue — S.L. Weiss
Variations — F. Sor
**II**
Chaconne — J.S. Bach
**III**
Fantasia — J. Turina
Tarantella — J. Turina
Granada — I. Albéniz
Torre Bermeja
Sevilla

**Wigmore Hall, London** 22 October 1937
**I**
Chaconne — Pachelbel
Allemande — J.S. Bach
Bourrée
Andante and Menuet — Haydn
Canzonetta — Mendelssohn

**II**
Prelude — Weiss
Allemande
Capriccio
Ballet
Sarabande
Gavotte
Gigue
**III**
Sonatina Meridional — Ponce
Tarantella — Castelnuovo-Tedesco
Serenata — Malats
Torre Bermeja — Albéniz

**Wigmore Hall, London 3** December 1938
**I**
Aria con Variazioni — Frescobaldi
Menuet — Rameau
Andante — Mozart
**II**
Prelude and Mazurka — Chopin
Choro No. 1 — Villa-Lobos

138

Guitarreo — Pedrell
Three Pieces — Granados
**III**
Variations on 'Folia de España' and Fugue —
Ponce
Six Catalan Folk Songs — arr. Llobet
Capriccio Diabolico (Omaggio a Paganini)
Op.85 — Castelnuovo-Tedesco

**Teatro Colón, Buenos Aires**
Autumn 1947
Preambulo — A. Scarlatti/M. Ponce
Sarabanda
Gavota
Sonata — D. Scarlatti
Aria Variada — G.F. Handel
Allegretto — J. Ph. Rameau
Minuetto — J. Haydn
Sonata (Omaggio a Boccherini)
— M. Castelnuovo-Tedesco
Fandanguillo — J. Turina
Tonadilla — E. Granados
Danza
Torre Bermeja — I. Albéniz
Sevilla

**Teatro Colón, Buenos Aires**
Autumn 1947
Aria Variada — G. Frescobaldi
Sonata Romántica — M. Ponce
Two Studies — H. Villa-Lobos
Tarantella — M. Castelnuovo-Tedesco
Fantasia — J. Turina
Antaño — O. Esplá
Danza in G — E. Granados
Estudio — F. Tárrega

**Teatro Colón, Buenos Aires**
Autumn 1947
**I**
Andante and Allegretto — F. Sor
Three Studies — F. Sor
Tema Variado — F. Sor
Sonatina in A — F. Moreno Torroba
**II**
Chaconne — J.S. Bach
**III**
Capriccio Diabolico Op.85 (Omaggio a
Paganini) — M. Castelnuovo-Tedesco
Mazurka — A. Tansman
Impresiones Ibéricas — M. Ponce
Granada — I. Albéniz
Leyenda

**Cambridge Theatre, London**
7 December 1947
Concerto in D Op.99 — Castelnuovo-
Tedesco
New London Orchestra
Conductor: Alec Sherman

Soloist: Andrés Segovia
(This was Segovia's first post-war appearance in Britain after an absence of nine
years).

**New York Town Hall, U.S.A.**
4 January 1948
**I**
Two Pieces — L. Milán
Passacaglia — L. Couperin
Lento e Allegretto — F. Sor
Sonata (Omaggio a Boccherini) Op. 77—
M. Castelnuovo-Tedesco
Allegro
Andantino quasi canzone
Tempo di Menuetto
Vivo ed energico
**II**
Siciliana — J.S. Bach
Fuga
Courante
Gavotte et Musette
Sarabande
Bourrée
Menuet
Gavotte en Rondeau
**III**
Sonatina — M. Ponce
Leyenda — I. Albéniz
Torre Bermeja
Sevilla

**New York Town Hall, U.S.A.**
7 March 1948
**I**
Aria con Variazioni — G. Frescobaldi
Two Sonatas — D. Scarlatti
Four Lute Pieces — S.L. Weiss
Chaconne — J.S. Bach
**II**
Mazurka — A. Tansman
Segovia — A. Roussel
Norteña — J.G. Crespo
Tarantella — M. Castelnuovo-Tedesco
Impromptu — C. Pedrell
Sevillana — J. Turina
Fandanguillo
Danza — E. Granados
Granada — I. Albéniz
Mallorca

**Bellas Artes, Mexico City** 1948
**I**
Chaconne — J.S. Bach
Allegretto — J.Ph. Rameau
Andante and Minuet — J. Haydn
Variations on a Theme by Mozart — F. Sor
**II**
Sonatina in A — F. Moreno Torroba
Impresiones Ibéricas — M. Ponce
Mallorca — I. Albéniz

139

*Sevilla*
*Prelude* — J.S. Bach
*Tremolo Study* — F. Tárrega

**Amsterdam** 1948
**I**
*Three Pieces* — H. Purcell
*Aria con Variazioni* — G.F. Handel
*Two Sonatas* — D. Scarlatti
*Andante and Allegretto* — J. Haydn
*Sonata* (Omaggio a Boccherini)
    — M. Castelnuovo-Tedesco
**II**
*Two Studies* — H. Villa-Lobos
*Fandanguillo* — J. Turina
*Tonadilla* — E. Granados
*Danza*
*Torre Bermeja* — I. Albéniz
*Leyenda*
*Sevilla*

**Amsterdam** 1948
**I**
*Sarabande variée* — G.F. Handel
*Preambulo et gavotte* — A. Scarlatti
*Sonata* — D. Scarlatti
*Passacaille* — L. Couperin
*Menueto* — J.Ph. Rameau
**II**
*Siciliana* — J.S. Bach
*Fuga*
*Corrente*
*Sarabande*
*Bourrée*
*Menueto*
*Gavota*
**III**
*Sonatina Meridional* — M. Ponce
    Campo
    Copla
    Fiesta
*Danza in G* — E. Granados
*Torre Bermeja* — I. Albéniz
*Sevilla*

**Edinburgh International Festival**
7 September 1948
**I**
*Preambule, Sarabande, Gavotte* — Scarlatti
*Sonata* — Scarlatti
*Allegretto* — Rameau
*Andante and Minuet* — Haydn
*Prelude* — J.S. Bach
*Fugue*
*Courante*
*Sarabande*
*Bourrée*
*Menuet*
*Gavotte en Rondeau*
**II**
*Norteña* — Crespo

140

*Mazurka* — Tansman
*Fandanguillo* — Turina
*Danza in E minor* — Granados
*Sevilla* — Albéniz

**Edinburgh International Festival**
September, 1948
**I**
*Two Pavanas* — Milán
*Prelude* — Weiss
*Allemande*
*Gavotte*
*Gigue*
*Passacaille* — Couperin
*Variations on a Theme by Mozart* — Sor
*Chaconne* — J.S. Bach
**II**
*Madroños* — Torroba
*Impresiones Ibéricas* — Ponce
*Tarantella* — Castelnuovo-Tedesco
*La Maja de Goya* — Granados
*Leyenda* — Albéniz

**Edinburgh International Festival**
10 September 1948
**I**
*Two Galliards* — Dowland
*Three Little Pieces* — Purcell
*Aria with Variations* — Handel
*Menuet* — Haydn
**II**
*Sonata in D* (Omaggio a Boccherini)   —
    Castelnuovo-Tedesco
**III**
*Two Studies* — Villa-Lobos
*Antaño* — Esplá
*Mazurka* — Ponce
*Danza No. 5* — Granados
*Mallorca* — Albéniz
*Torre Bermeja*

**Amsterdam** October 1949
**I**
*Two Pavanas* — L. Milán
*Suite in D minor* — R. de Visée
*Andante alla Siciliana* — F. Sor
*Allegro*
*Prelude* — S.L. Weiss
*Allemande*
*Allegramento*
*Ballet*
*Sarabande*
*Gavotte*
*Gigue*
**II**
*Canción y Danza* — M. Torroba
*Mazurka* — M. Ponce
*Segovia* — A. Roussel
*Tonadilla* — E. Granados
*Leyenda* — I. Albéniz

**The Hague** October 1949

**I**

*Three short pieces* — H. Purcell
  Irish Tune
  Menuet
  Gigue
*Aria con variazioni* — G.F. Handel
*Two Sonatas* — D. Scarlatti
*Andante en Allegretto* — J. Haydn

**II**

*Sonata* (Omaggio a Boccherini)
  — M. Castelnuovo- Tedesco
*Two Studies* — H. Villa-Lobos
*Fantasia* — J. Turina

**III**

*Tonadilla* — E. Granados
*Danza*
*Torre Bermeja* — I. Albéniz
*Leyenda*
*Sevilla*

**Amsterdam**, 1953
**Concertgebouw**
Wednesday 13 April
**Diligentia**
Thursday 14 April
**Riviera Hal**
Friday 15 April

**I**

*Suite in D* — Robert de Visée
  Allemande
  Bourrée
  Sarabande
  Courante
*Three Studies* — Fernando Sor
  in G
  in B flat
  in A
*Andantino and Allegro in D*
*Fandanguillo* — Joaquín Turina

**II**

*Passacaille* — Louis Couperin
*Prelude, Fugue and Gavotte* — Johann
  Sebastian Bach
*Minuetto* — Joseph Haydn
*Canzonetta* — Felix Mendelssohn

**III**

*Tonadilla* — Enrique Granados
*Danza in G*
*Torre Bermeja* — Isaac Albéniz
*Sevilla*

**Town Hall, Birmingham**
25 October 1953
City of Birmingham Symphony

Orchestra (Leader, Norris Stanley)
Conductor: Harold Gray

**I**

*Symphony No. 104 in D* (London) — Haydn

**II**

*Concerto in D for Guitar and Orchestra* —
  Castelnuovo-Tedesco
  (i)   Allegretto giusto e un poco pomposo
  (ii)  Andantino alla romanza
  (iii) Ritmico e cavalleresco
soloist: Segovia

Guitar Solos:
*Prelude and Loure* — Bach
*Menuet* — Rameau
*Tonadilla* — Granados
*Leyenda* — Albéniz

**III**

*Suite Pélleas and Mélisande* — Fauré
*Overture Cockaigne*, Op.40 — Elgar

**Ilkley Concert Club** King's Hall, Ilkley,
4 November 1953

**I**

*Aria con variazioni* — G. Frescobaldi
*Suite in A* — S.L. Weiss
  Prelude
  Ballet
  Sarabande
  Gigue
*Andante et Allegretto* — F. Sor

**II**

*Prelude et Loure* — J.S. Bach
*Sonata* — D. Scarlatti
*Allegretto* — J. Ph. Rameau
*Menuet*
*Canzonetta* — F. Mendelssohn

**III**

*Capriccio* (Homage to Paganini)
  — M. Castelnuovo-Tedesco
*La Maja de Goya* — E. Granados
*Mallorca* — I. Albéniz
*Torre Bermeja*

**Concertgebouw, Amsterdam**
6 November 1953

**I**

*Aria con variazioni* — Girolamo Frescobaldi
*Suite in A* — Silvius Leopold Weiss
  Prelude
  Allemande
  Allegramente
  Ballet
  Sarabande
  Gigue
*Gavotte* — Johann Sebastian Bach
*Cavatina* — Alexandre Tansman
  Prelude

Sarabande
Scherzino
Barcarolle
Danza Pomposa
**II**
*Two Studies* — Heitor Villa-Lobos
*Ricercare* — Mario Castelnuovo-Tedesco
*Tonadilla* — Enrique Granados
*Danza*
*Leyenda* — Isaac Albéniz

**Segovia Tour of USA and Canada 1954**
January 23 Independence, Mobil
January 24 Kansas City
January 29 Boulder, Colorado
January 31 New York (Television 'Toast of the Town')
February 1 Rapid City, South Dakota
February 6 Boston, Massachussetts
February 9 Meridian, Mississippi
February 11 Louisville, Kentucky
February 12 Nashville, Tennessee
February 17 Lexington, Virginia
February 20 New York Town Hall
February 23 Racine, Wisconsin
February 25 Houston, Texas
March 1 London, Canada
March 7 New York Town Hall
March 10 Pittsburg, Pennsylvania
March 12 Williamsburg, Virginia
March 16 Sarasota, Florida
March 18 Midland, Michigan
March 21 Chicago, Illinois
March 23 San Francisco, California
March 25 Watsonville, California
March 27 Arlington, West Virginia
March 29 Los Angeles, California
March 31 Victoria, Canada
April 3 Vancouver, Canada
April 4 Seattle, Oregon

**Boston Massachussetts** 6 February 1954
**I**
*Passacaglia* — Couperin
*Prelude* — J.S. Bach
*Sarabande*
*Loure*
*Allegretto and Menuet* — Rameau
*Canzonetta* — Mendelssohn
*Sonata in D* (Omaggio a Boccherini) — Castelnuovo-Tedesco
**II**
*Rondo* (Homage to Sor) — Ponce
*Fandanguillo* — Turina
*Inca Song and Improvisation* — Pedrell
*Danza in G* — Granados
*Mallorca* — Albéniz
*Sevilla*

**Amsterdam** 25 July 1954
**I**
*Passacaille* — Louis Couperin
*Menuet* — Jean Philippe Rameau
*Sicilienne* — Carl Phil. Em. Bach
*Prelude en Gavotte* — Joh. Seb. Bach
*Mallorca* — Isaac Albéniz
**II**
*Norteña* — Gomez Crespo
*Allegretto* — Moreno Torroba
*Dos Cantos populares Catalanas* — Miguel Llobet
*Sevilla* — Isaac Albéniz

**Royal Festival Hall, London**
28 October 1957
**I**
*Canción del Emperador* — L. de Narváez
*Two Galliards* — J. Dowland
*Preambulo and Gavotta* — A. Scarlatti/M. Ponce
*Sonata* — D. Scarlatti
*Fugue* — J.S. Bach
**II**
*Six Renaissance Lute Pieces* — arr. O. Chilesotti
*Introduction and Allegro* — F. Sor
*Three Studies* — H. Villa-Lobos
**III**
*Fantasia-Sonata* — J. Manén
*Three Danzas Levantinas* — O. Esplá
*Fandango* — J. Rodrigo
*Torre Bermeja* — I. Albéniz

**San Francisco Opera House** 5 March 1958
The San Francisco Symphony Orchestra
Conductor: Enrique Jordá
first performance of
*Fantasia para un Gentilhombre* — Joaquín Rodrigo
in the presence of the composer

**Royal Festival Hall, London**
Autumn 1958
**I**
*Fantasia* — Milán
*Pavana*
*Suite* — Roncalli
*Suite* — Weiss
*Prelude* — Bach
**II**
*Sonata Meridional* — Ponce
*Danza* — Rodrigo
*Suite* — Tansman
**III**
*Romance y Madroños* — Torroba
*Three Danzas Levantinas* — Esplá
*Sevilla* — Albéniz

142

**Segovia Tour of USA and Canada 1959**
March 1 Buffalo, New York
March 2 Niagara Falls, New York
March 3 Buffalo, New York
March 7 Washington D.C.
March 9 Durham, North Carolina
March 18 Berea, Kentucky
March 22 Boston, Massachussetts
March 29 Chicago, Illinois
April 2 Whittier
April 5 San Francisco
April 7 Sacramento
April 9 Berkeley
April 11 Los Angeles
April 15 Fort Worth
April 18 Midland, Texas
April 21 Wellesley, Massachussetts
April 22 Milton, Massachussetts
April 25 New York Town Hall
April 28 Toronto, Canada

August 24 — September 24 1959
**International Course on Spanish Music at Santiago de Compostella, Spain**
Tutors:
Composition:
  Oscar Esplá
  André Jolivet
  Federico Mompou
  Xavier Montsalvatge
  Joaquín Rodrigo
Ancient Spanish music:
  Mgr. Higinio Anglés
Interpretation:
  Singing: Victoria de los Angeles
  'Cello: Gaspar Cassadó
  Piano: José Iturbi
  Piano: Alicia de Larrocha
  Guitar: Andrés Segovia

**Segovia Tour of USA and Canada 1960**
January 4 Burlington, Vermont
January 6 Baltimore, Maryland
January 12 Ithaca, New York
January 15 Detroit, Michigan
January 16 Washington, D.C.
January 19 New London, Connecticut
January 21 Boston, Massachussetts
January 26 New Orleans, Louisiana
January 29 St. Petersburg, Florida
February 3 San Francisco, California
February 4 ''          ''          ''
February 5 ''          ''          ''
February 7 Stanford, California
February 9 Portland, Oregon
February 12 Seattle, Washington
February 14 Santa Monica, California
February 16 Los Angeles, California
February 18 Van Nuys, California
February 20 Monterey Park, California

February 23 San Diego, California
February 25 Manhattan, Kansas
February 28 Denver, Colorado
February 29 Scottsbluff, Nebraska
March 7 Ann Arbor, Michigan
March 13 Chicago, Illinois
March 19 Brooklyn, New York
March 21 Princeton, New Jersey
March 23 Westport, Connecticut
March 26 Rochester, New York
March 28 Buffalo, New York
April 1 Montclair, New Jersey
April 3 New Canaan, Connecticut
April 5 Syracuse, New York
April 7 Ottawa, Ontario, Canada
April 9 Hempstead, New York
April 12 Toronto, Canada
April 13 ''          ''
April 18 Watertown, Connecticut
April 25 Pittsburgh, Pennsylvania
April 27 Chapel Hill, North Carolina
April 29 Philadelphia, Pennsylvania

**Segovia Tour of USA and Canada 1961**
January 17 Akron, Ohio
January 20 Brooklyn, New York
January 23 Kingston, Ontario
January 27 New York Town Hall
February 1 Waterloo, Iowa
February 3–5 Pittsburgh, Pennsylvania
February 8 Belleville, Illinois
February 10 Detroit, Michigan
February 13–14 Nashville, Tennessee
February 16 Urbana, Illinois
February 18 New York Town Hall
February 21 Winston-Salem, North Carolina
February 23 Bowling Green, Kentucky
February 26 Chicago, Illinois
February 28 Minneapolis, Minnesota
March 2 Boulder, Colorado
March 4 Portland, Oregon
March 6 Walla Walla, Washington
March 8 Bakersfield, California
March 10 Los Angeles, California
March 12 Santa Monica, California
March 14 San Diego, California
March 16 Pasadena, California
March 19 San Francisco, California
March 21 Tucson, Arizona
March 23 Phoenix, Arizona
March 30 Montgomery, Alabama
April 1 Winter Park, Florida
April 3 Columbus, Georgia
April 5 Columbia, South Carolina
April 8 Washington D.C.
April 11 Oberlin, Ohio
April 13 Culver, Indiana
April 18 Baltimore, Maryland
April 20–21 University Park, Pennsylvania

April 23 Boston, Massachussetts
April 29 New York Town Hall

**Winter Park, Florida** 1 April 1961
*Pavanas* — L. Milán
*Suite in D* — R. de Visée
  Passacaille
  Bourrée
  Sarabande
  Menuet
  Gigue
*Rondo* — F. Sor
*Variations on a Theme by Mozart* — F. Sor
*Prelude* — J.S. Bach (arr. J. Duarte)
*Courante*
*Sarabande*
*Gigue*
*Largo assai and Menuet* — J. Haydn
*Two Songs Without Words* — F. Mendelssohn
*Zambra Granadina* — I. Albéniz
*Torre Bermeja*
*Granada*
*Leyenda*
*Mallorca*
*Sevilla*

**Royal Festival Hall** 30 May 1961
London Philharmonic Orchestra (Leader,
  Henry Datyner)
John Pritchard: conductor
Segovia: soloist
I
*The Spell of May* — Skalkottas
II
*Concerto in D for Guitar and Orchestra* —
  Castelnuovo-Tedesco
  Allegretto
  Andantino alla romanza
  Ritmico e cavalleresco
**Guitar Solos**: Segovia
*Allegro* — Sor
*Fandanguillo* — Turina
*Leyenda* — Albéniz
III
*Parade* — Satie

**Bath Festival, The Guildhall, Bath**
  4 June 1961
I
*Gaillardes* — Sanz
*Rondo and Allegro* — Sor
*Sonata* — Castelnuovo-Tedesco
II
*Prelude* — J.S. Bach
*Sarabande*
*Gigue*
*Menuet* — Schubert
*Canzonetta* — Mendelssohn
III
*Six Pieces* — Tansman

144

*Torre Bermeja* — Albéniz
*Leyenda*

**New Orleans Municipal Auditorium**
27 March 1962
New Orleans Philharmonic Symphony
  Orchestra
Conductor: James Yestadt
Soloist: Andrés Segovia
I
*Overture 'Semiramide'* — G. Rossini
II
*Concerto in E* — L. Boccherini (trans. G.
  Cassadó)
*Solos:*
*Suite* — R. de Visée
*Study* — F. Sor
*Sevilla* — I. Albéniz
III
*Symphony No.4 in F minor Op.36* — P.
  Tchaikowsky

**The Royal College of Music, London**
8 May 1962
I
*Three Pavanas (1535)* — L. Milán
*Study* — F. Sor
*Rondo*
*Canción y paisaje* — M. Ponce
*La fille aux cheveux de lin* — Debussy
II
*Sarabande and Gavotte* — Bach
*Two Sonatas* — Scarlatti
*Largo and Menuet* — Haydn
*Two Songs without words* — Mendelssohn
III
*Berceuse d'Orient* — Tansman
*Mazurka*
*Homage to Debussy* — Falla
*Two Preludes* — Villa-Lobos
*Romance y Madroños* — Torroba

**Pasadena Community Church,
St Petersburg, Florida** 24 January 1963
I
*Two Studies* — F. Sor
*Rondo*
*Romance* — F. Moreno Torroba
*Danza*
*Étude* — F. Tárrega
II
*Fantasia* — S.L. Weiss
*Bourrée* — J.S. Bach
*Menuet* — J.Ph. Rameau
*Sonata* — D. Scarlatti
III
*Melancolía; Canary's Flight; Arrulladora;
  Spring* from 'Platero y Yo' —
  M. Castelnuovo-Tedesco
*Sevillana* — J. Turina

Under the honorary chairmanship of Mrs John F Kennedy, the President's cabinet presents

**An Evening With Andrés Segovia State Department Auditorium, Washington D.C.** 18 March 1963

*Three Pieces* — Galilei
*Gavotte* — Bach
*Two Studies* — Sor
*Prelude in E* — Villa-Lobos
*Danza* — Granados
*Melancolía and Primavera* — Castelnuovo-Tedesco
*Romanza and Danza* — Torroba
*Torre Bermeja and Sevilla* — Albéniz

**Philharmonic Auditorium, Los Angeles, California** 22 March 1964
**I**
*Passacaglia* — L. Roncalli
*Giga*
*Gavotte*
*Prelude* — J.S. Bach
**II**
*Sonata Romántica* — (Homage à Schubert) M. Ponce
**III**
*Suite Compostellana* — F. Mompou
*Five Pieces* from 'Platero y Yo' — M. Castelnuovo-Tedesco
*Sevillana* (Fantasia) — J. Turina

**Royal Festival Hall, London**
20 May 1964
**I**
*Aria* — G.F. Handel
*Siciliana* — J.S. Bach
*Fugue*
*Gavotte*
*Romanza and Andante variato* — N. Paganini (arr. M. Ponce)
*Suite Compostellana* — F. Mompou
  1. Prelude
  2. Coral
  3. Cuna
  4. Recitativo
  5. Canción
  6. Muneira
**II**
*Sonata Romántica* (Hommage à Schubert) — M. Ponce
*Mallorca* — I. Albéniz
*Danza in G* — E. Granados

**Lounge Hall — Harrogate**
19 October 1965
**I**
*Five short pieces* — Purcell
*Andantino; Fughetta; Minuets;*

*Aria; Allegretto; Passepied* — Handel
*Introduction and Allegro* — Sor
**II**
*Suite in Modo Polonico* — Tansman
  Entrée; Gaillarde;
  Kujawiak; Tempo de Polonaise;
  Kolysanka No.1; Mazurka;
  Kolysanka No.2; Oberek
**III**
*Golondrinas; Ronsard; Primavera* — Castelnuovo-Tedesco
*Zambra Granadina* — Albéniz
*Torre Bermeja*
*Danza in G* — Granados

**Thames Hall, London, Ontario**
27 February 1966
**I**
*Five Little Pieces* — H. Purcell
*Sarabande and Bourrée* — J.S. Bach
*Thème varié* — F. Sor
**II**
*Study* — F. Tárrega
*Aria con variazioni and Allegretto* — G.F. Handel
*Gigue* — S.L. Weiss
*Mélodie* — E. Grieg
*Petite valse*
**III**
*Prelude in E minor* — H. Villa-Lobos
*Improvisation* — C. Pedrell
*Allegro Castellano* — F. Moreno Torroba
*Danza* — F. Mompou
*Sevilla* — I. Albéniz

**City Hall, Newcastle** 26 May 1967
**I**
*Fantasia and Pavana* — L. Milán
*Suite in D* — R. de Visée
  Entrée — Bourrée — Sarabande —
  Menuet — Passacaille — Courante
*Andante* — F. Sor
*Allegretto*
*Minueto*
*Rondo*
**II**
*Five short pieces* — H. Purcell
*Bourrée* — J.S. Bach
*Menuet* — F. Schubert
*Romanza and Andantino Variato* — N. Paganini
**III**
*Sonatina Meridional* — M. Ponce
  Campo — Copla — Fiesta
*Melancolía — Primavera — Arrulladora* — M. Castelnuovo-Tedesco
*Torre Bermeja* — I. Albéniz

145

**Musical Cruise on the new French liner 'Renaissance'**. May 1968
Artists include:
Amadeus String Quartet
Kempff
Menuhin
Milstein
Richter
Segovia
Stuttgart Chamber Orchestra

**Royal Festival Hall, London**
28 October 1968
I
*Six Pavanas* — L. Milán
*Aria con variazioni detta 'La Frescobalda'* — G. Frescobaldi
*Correntes*
*Siciliana* — J.S. Bach
*Bourrée*
*Song without Words* — F. Mendelssohn
*Canzonetta*
II
*Variations on a Theme of Handel* — Albert Harris
*Primavera* — M. Castelnuovo-Tedesco
*Cavatina* — A. Tansman
*English Suite* — John W. Duarte
*Mallorca* — I. Albéniz
*Torre Bermeja*

**Sweden**, 22 November 1968
I
*Six Pavanas* — L. Milán
*Aria con Variazioni; Corrente* — G. Frescobaldi
*Siciliana et Bourrée* — J.S. Bach
*Chanson et Canzonetta* — F. Mendelssohn
*Variations on a Theme of Handel* — A. Harris
*Primavera* — M. Castelnuovo-Tedesco
*Cavatina* — A. Tansman
  Prelude
  Sarabande
  Scherzino
  Barcarolle
  Danza Pomposa
II
*Mallorca* — I. Albéniz
*Torre Bermeja*
*Granada*
*Leyenda*
*Sevilla*

**Bushnell Memorial Auditorium, Hartford, Connecticut** 23 January 1969
I
*Introduction and Allegro* — F. Sor
*Two Studies* — F. Tárrega

*Two Preludes* — H. Villa-Lobos
*Madroños* — F. Moreno Torroba
II
*Suite in D* — R. de Visée
*Gavotte* — J.S. Bach
*Menuet* — J.Ph. Rameau
*Canzonetta* — F. Mendelssohn
III
*Melancolía* — M. Castelnuovo-Tedesco
*Primavera*
*Danza* — E. Granados
*Mallorca* — I. Albéniz
*Torre Bermeja*

**Constitution Hall, Washington DC**
29 March 1969
I
*Six Pavanas* — L. Milán
*Allemande* — J.S. Bach
*Sarabande*
*Bourrée*
*Allegro* — F. Sor
*Variations on a Theme of Handel* — A. Harris
II
*Suite 'Platero y Yo'* — M. Castelnuovo-Tedesco
(played in tribute to the memory of the composer)
*Cavatina* — A. Tansman
  Prelude
  Sarabande
  Scherzino
  Barcarolle
  Danza Pomposa
*Leyenda* — I. Albéniz

**Royal Festival Hall, London**
29 April 1970
I
*Canción del Emperador* — L.de Narvéz
*Diferencias sobre 'Guárdame las Vacas'*
*Castillos de España* — F. Moreno Torroba
*Four Pieces* — J. Dowland
*Sarabande and Variations* — G.F. Handel
*Minuet*
*Gavotte* — J.S. Bach
*Three Pieces* — E. Grieg
II
*Suite* — M. Castelnuovo-Tedesco (arr. Segovia)
*Prelude No.3* — H. Villa-Lobos
*Prelude No.1*
*Danzas Levantinas* — O. Esplá
*Torre Bermeja* — I. Albéniz

**Fairfield Hall, Croydon**, 18 May 1970
I
*Andante and Allegretto* — F. Sor
*Four short menuets* — F. Sor

146

*Introduction and Allegro*
*Theme with variations*
*Siciliana and Bourrée* — J.S. Bach
*Menuet* — S.L. Weiss
*Andante and Minueto* — J. Haydn
*Two Studies* — H. Villa-Lobos
**II**
*Sonatina Castellana* — F.M. Torroba
  Allegretto
  Andante
  Allegro
*Danza in E* — E. Granados
*Danza in G*
*Torre Bermeja* — I. Albéniz

**Birmingham Town Hall** 29 March 1971
**I**
*Suite* — R. de Visée
  Passacaille
  Gavotte
  Bourrée
  Menuet
  Courant
*Fandanguillo* — J. Turina
*Sonatina* — M. Ponce
  Campo, Copla, Fiesta
**II**
*Preambulo, Gavotta, Corrente* — A. Scarlatti
*Sonata* — D. Scarlatti
*Passacailla et Gaillarda* — G. Frescobaldi
*Siciliana, Fuga, Gavotte* — J.S. Bach
**III**
*English Suite* — J. Duarte
  Prelude
  Folk Song
  Round Dance
*Barcarola* — I. Albéniz
*Sevilla*

**Sweden** 11 November 1971
**I**
*Two Pieces for Vihuela* — L. de Narváez
*Allegretto grazioso* — F. Sor
*Andante*
*Allegretto*
*Castillos de España* — F. Moreno Torroba
  Turragana (Seranilla)
  Torija (Elegia)
  Manzanares del Real (A la moza fermosa)
  Montemayor (Contemplación)
  Alcaniz (Festiva)
  Alcazar de Segovia (Llamada)
**II**
*Two Galliards* — J. Dowland
*Sarabande* — J.S. Bach
*Bourrée*
*Gavotte*
*Three Sonatas* — D. Scarlatti

**III**
*From 'Suite in Modo Polonico'*
  — A. Tansman
  Kolisanka
  Mazurka
  Reverie
  Oberek
*Fantasia* — J. Turina
*Spanish Dance in E minor* — E. Granados
*Torre Bermeja* — I. Albéniz

**Toronto**, 13 Janury 1972
**I**
*Four Gaillardes* — John Dowland
  Melancolie
  Festive
  Melodie
  Rythme
*Three Sonatas* — Domenico Scarlatti
*Menuet* — Jean Philippe Rameau
*Theme with Variations* — Fernando Sor
**II**
*Suite in Modo Polonico* — Alexandre
  Tansman
  Kujawiak — Tempo di Polonaise —
  Reverie — Alla Polacca —
  Kolysanka II — Oberek
*Sonata (Omaggio a Boccherini)* — Mario
  Castelnuovo-Tedesco
  Allegro con spirito
  Andantino quasi canzone
  Tempo di minueto
  Vivo ed energico
**III**
*Two Levantine Impressions* — Oscar Esplá
*Fantasia* — Joquín Turina
*Mallorca* — Isaac Albéniz
*Torre Bermeja* )

**Symphony Hall, Boston**
Boston University Celebrity Series
27 February 1972
*Four Pieces* — J. Dowland
*Two Sonatas* — D. Scarlatti
*Variations on a Theme by Mozart* — F. Sor
*\*Movements from 'In Modo Polonico'*
  — A. Tansman
  Reverie
  Alla Polacca
  Kolysanka
  Mazurka
  Oberek
*\*Sonata in D (Omaggio a Boccherini) Op.77*
  — M. Castelnuovo- Tedesco
*\*Allegretto grazioso* — F. Moreno Torroba
*\*Fantasia* — J. Turina
*Mallorca* — I. Albéniz
*Torre Bermeja* — I. Albéniz
\*dedicated to Segovia

147

**Royal Festival Hall** October 1972
**I**
*Three Pavanas* — L. Milán
*Four Short Pieces* — J. Dowland
*Andantino* — G.F. Handel
*Aria*
*Allegretto*
*Rondo* — F. Sor
**II**
*Berceuse and Danse* — A. Tansman
*Sonata* (Omaggio a Boccherini) —
    M. Castelnuovo-Tedesco
    Allegro con spirito
    Andantino quasi canzona
    Tempo di minueto
    Vivo ed energico
**III**
*Sonata Mexicana* — M. Ponce
    (i)    Bailecito del Rebozo
    (ii)   Lo Que Suene el Ahuehuete
    (iii)  Ritmos y Cantos Aztecas
*Two Preludes* — H. Villa-Lobos
*Zambra Granadina* — I. Albéniz
*Torre Bermeja*

**Sweden** 16 November 1973
**I**
*Adagio, Courante* — S.L. Weiss
*Sonatina* — G. Benda
*Variations sur un thème populaire* — F. Sor
*Canción y Preludio* — F. Moreno Torroba
**II**
*Three Pieces* — G.F. Handel
*Two Sonatas* — D. Scarlatti
*Siciliana, Gavotte* — J.S. Bach
**III**
*Dipso* — V. Asencio
*Tarantella* — M. Castelnuovo-Tedesco
*Torre Bermeja* — I. Albéniz

**Royal Festival Hall** 4 October 1974
**I**
*Adagio e Corrente* — S.L. Weiss
*Andante in D* — F. Sor
*Variations on a Theme in D*
*Allegro in D*
*Tarantella* — M. Castelnuovo-Tedesco
**II**
*Sonatina* — G. Benda
*Prelude* — J.S. Bach
*Sarabande*
*Menuet*
*Gavotte en rondeau*
*Three Sonatas* — D. Scarlatti

**III**
*Diferencias on a Theme* — Munoz Molleda
*Dipso* — V. Asencio
*Serenata* — G. Samazeuilh
*Mallorca* — I. Albéniz

**Cambridge Guildhall** 11 October 1974
**I**
*Three Pavanas* — L. Milán
*Andante in C minor and Allegretto* — F. Sor
*Variations on a Theme in E minor*
*Danza in G* — E. Granados
**II**
*Sonata* — G.F. Handel
*Folia*
*Allegretto*
*Andante and Minuet* — J. Haydn
**III**
*Study and Prelude* — H. Villa-Lobos
*Barcarola and Danza Pomposa* — A. Tansman
*Melancolía y Golondrinas* — M. Castelnuovo-
    Tedesco
*Torre Bermeja* — I. Albéniz

**St. George's Hall Bradford**
7 November 1975
**I** ·
*Five Pieces from the XVI Century* — Anony-
    mous (arr. Chilesotti)
*Adagio and Gaillarda* — S.L. Weiss
*Two Mystic Compositions* — V. Asencio
*Fandanguillo* —Turina
**II**
*Five short pieces* — J.S. Bach
*Fugue*
*Gavotte*
**III**
*Andantino* — M. Castelnuovo-Tedesco
*Moderato* — *Stanco e sognante* — M. Castel-
    nuovo-Tedesco
*Fiesta* — M. Ponce
*Capricho* — I. Albéniz
*Sevilla*

**Royal Festival Hall** 30 October 1976
**I**
*Mille Regretz Canción del Emperador* —
    L. de Narváez
*Diferencias sobre Guárdame las Vacas*
*Pièces caractéristiques* — F.M. Torroba
*Danza in G* — E. Granados
**II**
*Prelude* — J.S. Bach
*Fugue*
*Bourrée*
*Largo assai*
*Allegretto*

**III**
*Berceuse d'Orient* — A. Tansman
*Danza Pomposa*
*Melancolía* — M. Castelnuovo-Tedesco
*Primavera*
*Granada* — I. Albéniz
*Leyenda*

**Royal Festival Hall** 28 March 1977
**I**
*Suite in D* — R. de Visée
*Andante* — F. Sor
*Allegro*
*Menuet*
*Rondo*
*Folias, with variations* — F. Sor
**II**
*Aria and Allegretto* — Handel
*Prelude, Fugue, Sarabande* — Bach
**III**
*Sonatina* — F.M. Torroba
   *Allegretto*
   *Andante*
   *Allegro*
*Two Pieces* — A. Tansman
*Two Danzas* — E. Granados

**Free Trade Hall, Manchester**
5 October 1977
**I**
*Three Studies:*
   B flat; A minor; E minor — F. Sor
*Introduction, Theme and Variations in E minor*
*Sonata in D* — M. Ponce
*Spring* — M. Castelnuovo-Tedesco
**II**
*Menuet* — Schubert
*Six short pieces* — Schumann
*Canzonetta* — Mendelssohn
**III**
*Suite Mistica* — Asencio
*Torre Bermeja* — Albéniz
*Sevilla*
*Leyenda*

**Free Trade Hall, Manchester**
25 October 1978
**I**
*Song of the Emperor and Variations on a*
   *Spanish popular tune* — L. de Narváez
*Andante, Menuet, Rondo* — F. Sor
*Five Pieces from 'Platero and I'*
   — M. Castelnuovo-Tedesco
   Prelude — Tempo de Habanera
   Kolisaro — Melancolía — Primavera
**II**
*Prelude* — *Siciliana* — *Corrente* — J.S. Bach
*Sonata* — D. Scarlatti

*Andante and Allegretto in D* — J. Haydn
**III**
*Sonatina Meridional* — M. Ponce
   Campo — Copla — Fiesta
*La Maja de Goya* — E. Granados
*Sevilla* — I. Albéniz

President and Mrs Carter
Honor Andrés Segovia
**A Concert at The White House**
11 March 1979
Program
*Song of the Emperor and 'Diferencias' on a*
   *Spanish Tune* — L. de Narváez
*Fugue (Originally for lute)* — J.S. Bach
*Theme and Variations* — F. Sor
*Menuet in A*
*Melancoliá (Dolce e Mesto)* —
   M. Castelnuovo-Tedesco
*Primavera (Quasi Toccata)*
*Allegretto Castellano* — F. Moreno Torroba
*Sevilla* — I. Albéniz

**Royal Festival Hall** 13 October 1979
**I**
*Six Renaissance lute pieces*
   — arr. O. Chilesotti
*Prelude and Fugue* — J.S. Bach
*Two Sonatas* — D. Scarlatti
*Three short compositions* — E. Grieg
**II**
*Suite in Modo Polonico* — A. Tansman
   Entrée — Gaillarde — Kujawiak —
   Tempo de Polonaise — Kolysanka No.1
   Mazurka — Reverie — Alla Polacca —
   Kolysanka No.2 — Oberek
**III**
*Suite mistic* — V. Asencio
   Moderato — Lento — Allegretto
*Fantasia* — J. Turina
*Granada* — I. Albéniz
*Capricho*
*Sevilla*

All the works in tonight's programme have
been revised and adapted for the guitar by
Segovia.

**Seattle Opera House** 20 January 1980
**I**
*Five Pieces from the Renaissance*
   — arr. O. Chilesotti
*Sarabande and Allegretto* — G.F. Handel
*Sonata* — D. Scarlatti
*Two Menuets* — J. Haydn
*Romanza and Capriccio* — N. Paganini

**II**
*Suite in Modo Polonico* — A. Tansman
    Entrée — Gaillarde — Kujawiak —
    Tempo de Polonaise — Kolysanka No.1
    Reverie — Mazurka — Alla Polacca —
    Kolysanka No.2 — Oberek
**III**
*Sonatina* — F.M. Torroba
    Allegretto grazioso
    Andante espressivo
    Allegro ritmico
*Fandanguillo* — J. Turina
*Capricho Arabe* — F. Tárrega
*Torre Bermeja* — I. Albéniz

**Free Trade Hall Manchester**
8 October 1980
**I**
*Suite in D* — de Visée
*Aria con Variazioni* — Frescobaldi
*Three Pieces* — Haydn
**II**
*Sonata Mexicana* — Ponce
*Barcarola and Danza Pomposa from 'Cavatina'*
    — Tansman
*Two Preludues* — Villa-Lobos
**III**
*Three Levantine Impressions* — Esplá
*Capricho* — Tárrega
*Danza* — Granados
*La Maja de Goya*
*Leyenda* — Albéniz

**Royal Festival Hall** 18 October 1981
**I**
*Andante and Allegro in C* — F. Sor
*Theme and Variations in B*
*Sonatina Meridional* — M. Ponce
    1. Campo   2. Copla   3. Fiesta
**II**
*Passacaille and Corrente* — G. Frescobaldi
*Aria and Minuet* — G.F. Handel

*Two Sonatas* — D. Scarlatti
*Minueto* — F. Schubert
**III**
*Reverie and Mazurka* — A. Tansman
*Two Mediterranean Impressions* — O. Esplá
*Sonatina in A* — F. Torroba
    Allegretto grazioso
    Andante espressivo
    Allegro ritmico

**British Tour 1982**
  2   October  Rochdale
  5   October  Swansea
  9   October  Reading
11   October  Croydon
20   October  Warwick University
23   October  Barbican, London
29   October  Telford, Shropshire

Andrés Segovia First Concert British Tour
October 1982
**Gracie Fields' Theatre, Rochdale**
Saturday 2 October 1982
**I**
*Andante* — F. Sor
*Allegretto*
*Allegro*
*Five Studies* — F. Sor
*Six short connected pieces* — F. Tárrega
**II**
*Siciliana* — J.S. Bach
*Siciliana* — C.P.E. Bach
*Two Menuets* — J.P. Rameau
*Andante & Allegretto* — J. Haydn
**III**
*Sonata Mexicana* — M. Ponce
    Allegro moderato
    Intermezzo
    Andante espressivo
    Allegro ritmico
*Mallorca* — I. Albéniz
*Sevilla*

President and Mrs. Carter
Honor
Andrès Segovia

*A Concert
at
The White House*

Sunday, March 11, 1979

*Program*

| | |
|---|---|
| Song of the Emperor and Diferencias on a Spanish Tune * | L. de Narvaez (Ca. 1538) |
| Fugue (Originally for Lute) * | J. S. Bach (1685-1750) |
| Theme and Variations Menuet in A | F. Sor (1778-1839) |
| Melancolia (Dolce e Mesto) Primavera (Quasi Toccata) | M. Castelnuovo-Tedesco (1895-1968) |
| Allegretto Castellano | F. Moreno Torroba (Born 1891) |
| Sevilla * | I. Albeniz (1860-1909) |

*Revised and adapted by Andrès Segovia*

Programme of the White House recital, 11 March 1979. (Courtesy the Carter White House Photo Office.)

Andrés Segovia plays at the White House, 11 March 1982.
(Photo: courtesy the Carter White House Photo Office. Collection, Carter Presidential Materials Project.)

# SELECT
# BIBLIOGRAPHY

*Books by Segovia*
**Segovia, Andrés**: *Segovia, an autobiography of the years 1893–1920*, Macmillan, New York, 1976 and Marion Boyars, London, 1976.
*Segovia, my book of the guitar*, Collins, New York, 1979.

*Books about Segovia*
**Bobri, Vladimir:** *The Segovia Technique*, Macmillan, New York, 1972.
**Clinton, George:** *Andrés Segovia, An Appreciation*, Musical New Services, London 1978.
**Gavoty, Bernard:** *Segovia, Great Concert Artists*, René Kister, Geneva, 1955.
**Purcell, Ronald C.:** *Andrés Segovia, Contributions to the World of Guitar*, Belwin Mills, New York, 1975.

*Books about the Classical Guitar*
**Bellow, Alexander:** *The Illustrated History of the Guitar*, Colombo, New York, 1970.
**Bone, Philip J.:** *The Guitar and Mandolin*, reprint of 2nd edition, Schott, London, 1972.
**Duncan, Charles:** *The Art of Classical Guitar Playing*, Summy-Birchard Music, Princeton, 1980.
**Evans, Tom & Mary:** *Guitars, From the Renaissance to Rock*, Paddington Press, London, 1977.
**Ed. Ferguson, J.:** *The Guitar Player Book*, Grove Press, New York, 1978.
**Giertz, Martin:** *Den Klassika Gitarren*, Norstedt, Stockholm, 1979.
**Grunfeld, Frederic V.:** *The Art and Times of the Guitar*, Macmillan, New York 1969.
**Mairants, Ivor:** *My Fifty Fretting Years*, Ashley Mark, Gateshead, 1980.
**Summerfield, Maurice J.:** *The Classical Guitar, Its Evolution and its Players since 1800*, Ashley Mark, Gateshead, 1982.
**Turnbull, Harvey:** *The Guitar from the Renaissance to the Present Day*, London, Batsford, 1974.
**Wade, Graham:** *Traditions of the Classical Guitar*, London, John Calder 1980.
*Your Book of the Guitar*, Faber and Faber, London 1980.

*Books about Flamenco and Spanish Music*
**Fajardo, Eduardo Molina:** *El Flamenco en Granada, Teoría de sus Orígenes e Historia*, Miguel Sanchez, Granada 1974.
**Grande, Felix:** *Memoria del Flamenco, I & II*, Espasa-Calpe, S.A., Madrid 1979.
**Pohren, D.E.:** *Lives and Legends of Flamenco, A Biographical History*, Society of Spanish Studies, Madrid 1964, reissued Musical New Services, Shaftesbury, 1983
*The Art of Flamenco*, Society of Spanish Studies, Sevilla, 1962, reissued Musical New Services, Shaftesbury, 1983.
**Triana, Fernando el de:** *Arte y Artistas Flamencos*, Ediciones Córdoba, Demófilo, 1978.

**Chase Gilbert:** *The Music of Spain*, Dover Publications, New York 1941.
**Livermore, Ann:** *A Short History of Spanish Music*, Duckworth, London 1972.

*Books about Spanish Composers*
**Manuel de Falla**
Burnett James: *Manuel de Falla & the Spanish Musical Renaissance*, Gollancz, London, 1979.
Jaime Pahissa: *Manuel de Falla, His Life and Works*, Museum Press, London, 1954.
ed. Federico Sopeña; *Manuel de Falla, On Music and Musicians*, Marion Boyars, London, 1979.
J.B. Trend: *Manuel de Falla and Spanish Music*, Alfred A. Knopf, New York, 1929.
**Joaquín Rodrigo**
Vicente Vayá Plá: *Joaquín Rodrigo, Su Vida y Su Obra*, Real Musical, Madrid, 1977.
**Joaquín Turina**
J.L. García del Busto: *Turina*, Espasa-Calpe, S.A., Madrid, 1981.